CHAPTER ONE

SHE WAS A THIEF.

A thief...

Jasmine Nichols's heart pounded the indictment through her bloodstream. She hadn't stolen anything yet, but that was beside the point. She'd travelled thousands of miles for the sole purpose of taking something that didn't belong to her.

Telling herself she had no choice didn't matter. If anything, it escalated her helplessness.

By the end of the night, she would wear the damning label as close to her skin as her black designer evening gown clung now.

Because failure wasn't an option.

Fear and shame duelled for supremacy inside her, but it was the deep knowledge that she couldn't turn her back on her family that propelled her reluctant feet up the sweeping crimson carpet towards the awe-inspiring masterpiece that housed the Contemporary Museum of Arts, perched on a cliff-side overlooking Rio de Janeiro. Even the jaw-dropping beauty of her surroundings couldn't detract her from the simple fact.

She'd come here to steal.

The smile she'd plastered on her face since alighting from the air-conditioned limo threatened to crack. To calm her nerves, she mentally recited her *to do* list.

First, she had to locate Crown Prince Reyes Vicente Navarre.

And there was her first problem.

All effective search engines had yielded no pictures of the reclusive prince, save for a grainy image taken at the funeral of his mother four years ago. Since then, no pictures of the royal family of the South American kingdom of Santo Sierra had been released to the public. They guarded their privacy with a rigour that bordered on fanaticism.

As if that weren't bad enough, according to reports, the House of Navarre's Crown Prince had left his kingdom only three times in the last three years, all his time spent caring for his gravely ill father. It was rumoured King Carlos Navarre wasn't expected to live past the summer.

Which meant Jasmine had no means of identifying Prince Reyes Navarre.

How did she get close to a man whose identity she had no idea of, distract him long enough to get her hands on what she'd come for before her mother and, more importantly, her stepfather, Stephen Nichols, the man who'd saved her life, and whose name she'd adopted, found out what she was up to?

Stephen would be heartbroken if he knew she was being blackmailed.

A nerve-destroying shudder rose up from the soles of her feet, making her clench her teeth to stop its death rattle from escaping. She smiled some more, mingled with the insanely wealthy and well heeled, and tried to reassure herself she could do this. By this time tomorrow, she'd be back home.

And most importantly, Stephen would be safe.

If everything went smoothly.

Stop it! Negative thinking was the downfall of many a plan. How many times had Stephen told her this?

She fixed her wilting smile back in place, stepped into the main hall of the museum, but she couldn't summon the enthusiasm to gawp at the stunning paintings and sculptures on display.

A waiter approached bearing a tray of champagne. Accepting the sparkling gold-filled crystal goblet, she smoothed a shaky hand over the pearl choker around her throat, ignored the nervous flutter in her belly, and made her way to the bowl-shaped terrace where the guests were congregating for pre-dinner drinks.

So far the plans set out by Joaquin Esteban—the man threat-

MARRIED FOR THE PRINCE'S CONVENIENCE

BY
MAYA BLAKE

MILLS BOON

Published in Great Britain 2015
by Mills & Boon, an imprint of Harlequin (UK) Limited,
Eton House, 18-24 Paradise Road, Richmond, Surrey, TW9 1SR

© 2015 Maya Blake

ISBN: 978-0-263-24880-7

Harlequin (UK) Limited's policy is to use papers that are natural,
renewable and recyclable products and made from wood grown in
sustainable forests. The logging and manufacturing processes conform
to the legal environmental regulations of the country of origin.

Printed and bound in Spain
by CPI, Barcelona

MARRIED FOR THE PRINCE'S CONVENIENCE

ening her stepfather's life—had gone meticulously. Her name had been on the guest list as promised, alongside those of world leaders and celebrities she'd only seen on TV and in glossy magazines. For a single moment, while she'd waited for Security to check the electronic chip on her invitation, she'd secretly hoped to be caught, turned away. But the man who held her stepfather's fate in his cruel hands had seen to every last detail she needed to pull this off.

Everything except provide her with a picture of the thirty-two-year-old prince.

The first stage of the treaty signing was to take place in half an hour in the Golden Room behind her. And with the occasion coinciding with Prince Mendez of Valderra's birthday, guests had been invited onto the terrace to witness the spectacular sunset and the prince's arrival, before the signing and birthday celebrations began.

Crown Prince Reyes himself was expected at eight o'clock. A quick glance at her watch showed five minutes to the hour. With every interminable second that ticked by, Jasmine's nerves tightened another notch.

What if she was found out? Certainly, she could kiss her job as a broker and mediator goodbye. But even if she succeeded, how could she ever hold her head high again? She'd worked so very hard to put her past behind her, to tend the new leaf she'd turned over. For eight years, she'd succeeded. And now, at twenty-six, she was on the slippery slope again.

Because once a juvie princess, always a juvie princess?

No. She hadn't let that voice of her detention cellmate taunt her for years. She wasn't about to start now.

And yet, she couldn't stop the despair that mingled with anxiety as her gaze drifted over the orange-splashed water towards the stunning silhouette of Sugarloaf Mountain in the distance.

Under normal circumstances, the sights and sounds would have filled her with excitement and awe. For a girl with her past and dire upbringing, sights such as these didn't feature in her *normal*. Except these weren't normal circumstances. And fear was threatening to block out every other emotion.

Which was dangerous. She couldn't afford to fail. Yet success would bring nothing but shame. Would prove that the past really never stayed in the past.

But the reality was her stepfather had gone too far this time, hedged his bets, literally, with the wrong person.

Joaquin, with his soft voice and deadly smile, had calmly given her two choices.

Come to Rio or watch Stephen rot in jail.

Of course, Joaquin had counted on the fact that, aside from his very public humiliation of being thrown out of his Foreign Office position for gambling away government money, Stephen Nichols's devotion to his wife meant he would do anything to save her the distress of watching him suffer. As would Jasmine.

Even when Jasmine was a child, long before Stephen had entered their lives, her mother's fragility had meant she had assumed the role of the caretaker. Her mother wouldn't survive losing Stephen.

So here Jasmine was, about to step into a quagmire she wasn't sure any amount of self-affirmation would wash her clean of.

'He's here!'

She roused herself from her maudlin self-pitying. A quick glance showed it was precisely eight o'clock. Her heart double somersaulted into her throat. When her stomach threatened to follow suit, she took a hasty sip of champagne. Whatever Dutch courage she hoped to gain was sorely lacking as the butterflies in her stomach grew into vicious crows.

Following the direction of excited voices and pointing, she focused on the bottom of the cliff. A sleek speedboat approached, foaming waves billowing behind the fast-moving craft. It gathered speed as it neared the shore. Swerving at the last second, it created a huge arc of water that rushed to the shore in a giant wave before heading away from the jetty.

The pilot executed a series of daredevil manoeuvres that

brought gasps of delight from the crowd and left the other two occupants—bodyguards, judging by their bulging muscles and ill-fitting suits—clinging grim-faced to the sides.

Finally, bringing the vessel alongside the quay, the tuxedoed figure stepped boldly onto the bow of the boat and jumped lithely down onto the jetty. Smiling at the enthusiastic applause, he clasped his hands in front of him and gave a deep bow.

Jasmine released the breath trapped in her lungs. So, this was Prince Reyes Navarre. Considering his near reclusive status, she was surprised he'd chosen such a narcissistic, highly OTT entrance. She wrinkled her nose.

'You're not impressed with His Royal Highness's maritime prowess?' a deep voice enquired from behind her left shoulder.

Jasmine jumped and whirled around. She'd assumed she was alone on the terrace, everyone else having rushed down into the main hall to welcome the prince.

How had this man moved so silently behind her? She hadn't even felt his presence until he'd spoken. Jasmine's gaze raced up, and up, until it collided with dark grey eyes.

Immediately, she wanted to look away, to block the probing gaze. She had no idea why, but the urge was so overwhelming, she took a step back.

A strong hand seized her arm. 'Careful, *pequeña*. It is a long tumble from the terrace and the evening is too beautiful to mar with tragedy.'

Glancing behind her, she realised she'd stepped dangerously close to the low wall bordering the terrace.

'Oh. Thank you.' Her words twisted around her tongue. Her senses dovetailed on the warm hand that held her. She looked down at the elegant fingers on her skin and drew in a sharp breath. His bold touch transmitted an alien sensation through her blood.

As if he felt it too, his fingers tightened imperceptibly. A second later, he let go. 'So, you don't like speedboats?' He nodded over her head at the spectacle below.

She tried to pry her gaze from his face, but she only succeeded in moving her head a fraction, before becoming equally hypnotised by the alluring spectacle of his mouth.

It was just spectacularly…sensual. Like his eyes, the lines of his lips drew equal interest from her stunned senses. Without stopping to assess her reaction, she found herself raising her hand to his face.

A hair's breadth away, she saw his eyes widen. Her heart slammed with horror and embarrassment at what she'd almost done. She snatched her hand back and for a split second contemplated taking that fatal step backwards. Maybe dashing herself over the rocks at the bottom of the cliff would knock some sense into her.

'What makes you say that?' she prevaricated when it became clear he expected an answer to his question.

'You have a very expressive face.' His beautifully deep accented voice was solemn.

'Oh.' She stalled and tried to think fast. What could she say without causing offence? 'They're okay, I guess. I mean, they're not my thing. Too fast. Too…wet.' Not to mention, they reminded her of the times Stephen had taken her out on his boat very soon after she and her mother had gone to live with him. Still in her destructive phase, she'd given him a hard time about those trips. Despite his many reassurances, a part of her had remained untrusting, afraid he'd end up being like all the men her mother had fallen for in the past. Each morning, she'd woken up anxious that that would be the day Stephen tossed them out of his life. He hadn't, of course, but she still couldn't look at a boat without remembering that distressing period. 'But they're nice to look at, I suppose.' She bit her lip to stop further inanity spilling out.

The stranger's grave nod did nothing to distract her stare. 'But exhilarating, some would say. No?'

Light-headedness encroached. Exhilarating. Breath-stealing. Captivating. But all those adjectives had nothing to do with speedboats and everything to do with the man in front of her.

Belatedly, Jasmine realised she hadn't taken a single breath since she'd clapped eyes on him. Sucking in oxygen restored some much-needed brain activity. 'I wouldn't know. I've never been inclined to take a trip on one. Mainly because I get seasick standing on a beach.'

'That's a shame. There is a tranquillity I find on water that I haven't found anywhere else.'

The thought of this man, powerfully built, quietly commanding and confident, craving tranquillity touched a strange place inside her.

'My stepfather loves the water too.' Damn. She needed to watch her tongue.

'But something about it makes you sad?' His voice softened as his eyes grew even more solemn.

Her startled gaze flew to his. 'Why do you say that?'

'You speak with fondness but your eyes darken with unhappiness.'

His intuitiveness disturbed her, made her feel vulnerable. Wrenching her gaze from his, she looked around. The terrace was deserted, but soft lights glowed from exquisite crystal-cut chandeliers and showed the guests slowly filling the large hall.

The hall...

Where she should be. Trying to make contact with Prince Reyes Navarre.

Instead she was alone with this strangely captivating man.

A man she didn't know.

Although she'd talked herself into believing not every stranger meant her harm, she knew better than most which situations to avoid. Being alone with a man twice her size wasn't a good idea.

But rather than fear, a thrum of excitement fizzed through her veins. Her breathing constricted, her heart thumping loud in her ears as she inhaled. Almost drawn by an invisible force, her gaze returned to his face.

His black dinner jacket and crisp white shirt gave his features a vibrancy, helped in no small measure by the golden perfection of his skin. Cast in part shadow by the broad shoulders blocking the light, his taut cheekbones and strong, un-compromising jaw made her fingers tingle with the urge to explore him.

As she stared his mouth hardened into a tight line, as if he held some emotion in. The strong need to touch those lips, experience their firm texture and soothe them softer with her thumb grew. Her eyes flashed back to his to find him regarding her, waiting for a response.

'I have issues with water. Let's just leave it at that.'

He looked as if he would demand more. But he merely nodded. 'Tell me your name.' His authoritative tone demanded nothing but her compliance.

Without questioning why, she answered, 'Jasmine Nichols.'

His solemn expression altered, fleetingly replaced by a small smile that creased his lips. 'You are named after the flower that blooms in the gardens of my home, Jasmine.' His voice caressed her name in a way that made all the hairs on her body strain to life. 'It is a fragile yet sturdy flower that has soothed us with its heady fragrance for thousands of years.'

Overwhelmed by the equally heady blend of emotion swirling through her, she gave a nervous laugh. 'Blimey, I hope I don't look that old!'

'Be assured. You don't.'

His smile disappeared, but she suspected he was still amused by her. The thought created a joyous fizz in her blood. It struck her that this man, whoever he was, hadn't smiled or laughed in a long time. The urgent need to catch another glimpse of that enigmatic smile grew.

'Great. Living to a thousand sounds like fun, but I bet it becomes a nuisance after that. A few more decades will do me just fine, though. I have things to do, people to impress.'

Joy sang in her chest when he rewarded her with another fleeting smile.

'I have no doubt that you will make your mark on the world before you leave it.' His head dipped in a shallow bow. 'Enjoy the rest of your evening, Jasmine.' With graceful, long-limbed strides, he walked away from her.

His abrupt departure stunned her into stillness. She watched four figures detach themselves from the shadowed doorway and fall into step behind him. She didn't need to be told they were bodyguards.

And rightly so. He was far too lethal to walk around without armed escort.

It wasn't until he reached the bottom of the stairs that led into the main hall that she regained the power of speech.

'Holy hotness, Batman,' she muttered under her breath, still more than a little stunned.

Watching him cut a path through the assembled crowd, Jasmine realised she hadn't even asked his name. Without pausing to think, she dashed through the doors after him.

She came to a screeching halt after a few steps.

What was she doing? She hadn't come to Rio to check out its male citizens, or to fall flat on her face for the first enigmatic man who looked at her with deep, hypnotically solemn eyes.

The real reason wrenched her back to reality, making any dream she harboured glaringly impossible. Whoever the mysterious, formidable stranger was, he had nothing to do with her mission here.

A mission that should've been the one and only thing on her mind.

She slid her wrap closer to ward off the sudden chill invading her body.

How could she have lost sight of her objective so quickly? Her stepfather's well-being depended on her. Running after a man who'd made her feel so alive, so special that she would have given up all she held dear to spend another minute in his presence was out of the question.

She clutched her grey silk purse and tried to think clearly, but it was no use. His smell, the feel of his hand on her skin, the intensity of his dark gaze that seemed to see past the outer trappings of civilised conversation to her inner self, remained imprinted on her.

Her breath rushed out shakily. She tried to tell herself what she'd felt didn't matter. That wasn't her purpose here. The only thing that mattered was finding Prince Reyes, getting her hands on the treaty and making it out of here in one piece. By way of grounding herself, she recited the list once more and forced herself to move into the hall as she did so.

The first thing she noticed was that the man she'd been speaking to was now on the other side of the room. Similarly suited men surrounded him, yet he remained curiously aloof, standing out so spectacularly, everyone else faded into insignificance.

Forcing her gaze away, she looked around. In halting Portuguese, she tried to enquire discreetly from her waiter which of the men was Prince Reyes, but her query only drew a blank stare.

Her anxiety returned when she realised most of the conversation going on around her was in Portuguese. Naïvely, she'd assumed since most of the staff at her hotel spoke English, everyone in Rio did too.

But the man who'd spoken to her on the terrace had used perfect English.

So ask him.

Except she couldn't. She'd have to cross the room to get to him, and in the time she'd been dithering his audience had tripled.

Insinuating herself into his crowd would only draw attention to herself. And for what she'd come here to do, anonymity was key. Wishing she'd pressed Joaquin Esteban for more details about the prince, she cast another look around.

A bell sounded nearby, making her jump. Guests started taking their places at the long banquet table. She found her place and had just sat down when a light-haired man joined her.

He looked at her hopefully. 'Please tell me you speak English?'

Jasmine smiled with relief. 'Yes, I do.'

'Thank God! You think your Portuguese is all right until someone asks you a question. Then even the little you know flies straight out of your head. I'm Josh, by the way.'

'Jasmine,' she responded.

'Crazy, isn't it?'

Startled, Jasmine glanced sideways to him. 'Sorry?'

He nodded to the group of men taking their seats at the far end of the long banquet table. 'Unbelievable that between the two of them, those men control nearly half of the steel and precious gems in the world.'

Unwilling to disclose her ignorance, she murmured, 'Right.'

'Shame their trade relations are in a shambles, though. Hopefully once the treaty is signed, there should be some semblance of order, otherwise the chaos will only get worse.' He shook his head. 'Prince Reyes has done an outstanding job of bringing the treaty to fruition, though. Have to commend him on that.' He took a healthy gulp of champagne.

Sneaking in a breath to calm her screeching nerves, she casually asked, 'Which one is Prince Reyes?'

He looked puzzled for a second, then he shrugged. 'I understand how you might be confused. They're descended from the same bloodline, after all.' He nodded to the men. 'Mendez, the shorter one who rocked up in the speedboat, is the birthday boy celebrating the big four-oh. He's in charge of Valderra, the larger of the two kingdoms. The taller one at the head of the table, talking to the prime minster, is Reyes. Don't get me wrong, his might be the smaller of the kingdoms, but Santo Sierra is definitely the big kahuna.'

Jasmine's throat threatened to close up as she absorbed the information. Her fingers clenched around her cutlery as ice drenched her blood.

The lights went up just then and two officious-looking men stepped up to the twin podiums carrying black briefcases. Heart in her throat, she realised what she'd done.

She'd been speaking to Prince Reyes Navarre all along!

And she'd told him her name!

After a short speech, the first stage of the treaty signing was completed. Jasmine watched as the documents were placed back in the briefcases.

Clammy sweat soaked her palms. Carefully, she set down her knife and fork. Every instinct told her to get up. *Run.* Not stop until she was on the next plane back to London.

But how could she? Even if she sold her two-bedroom East London flat and somehow found the balance to pay the half a million pounds owed to Joaquin, the loan shark still possessed enough documentary evidence to bury her stepfather.

Jasmine's heart lurched at the thought. Her family was far from perfect, but Stephen Nichols had single-handedly ensured she and her mother had been given a much-needed second chance. There was no way Jasmine was going to turn her back on him now.

Nervously, she swallowed the moisture in her mouth. 'You mean, Prince Reyes is the tall one…' *with the impossibly broad shoulders, sad eyes and expressive, elegant hands*, she nearly blurted out.

'Looking our way right now,' her table companion muttered, a vein of surprise trailing his voice.

Her head jerked up and slate-grey eyes locked on hers. Even from the length of the banquet table, the stranger from the terrace loomed larger than life, his stare unwavering.

Except he wasn't an intriguing stranger any more.

He was the man she'd come to steal from.

CHAPTER TWO

Shame should have been the paramount emotion ruling Jasmine as her gaze remained trapped in Prince Reyes's stare.

Instead, the alien emotion from earlier pulsed through her again, and, impossibly, everything and everyone seemed to fade away. Even the sound of her own breathing slowed until she barely knew whether she breathed in or out.

Alarmed and more than a little unsettled, Jasmine wrenched her gaze away. All through the meal she barely tasted, she forced herself to make light conversation with Josh. But even with her focus firmly turned away from Prince Reyes, she could feel his stare, heavy and speculative, on her.

Now, realising just how precarious a position she'd put herself in, Jasmine was barely able to hold it together. Which was why she didn't hear Josh clear his throat.

Once. Twice.

Her gaze jerked up to find Prince Reyes Navarre standing next to her. Startled, she dropped the knife and cringed as it clattered onto her plate.

'Miss Nichols, was your meal satisfactory?' He glanced pointedly at her half-eaten meal.

Aware of the countless pairs of eyes on her, Jasmine wasn't sure whether to remain seated or stand and curtsy. She opted to remain seated. 'Y-yes, it was, thank you.'

'I am not interrupting, I hope?' A glance at Josh that was at once courteous and incisive.

'No, we're…just two countrymen who find themselves at the same table.' Josh laughed.

'How…fortunate,' Prince Reyes said, his gaze speculative as it rested on the other man.

Vaguely, she saw him gesture. Suddenly, the guests rose

from their places and started to mingle. Sensing some sort of etiquette being observed, Jasmine stood shakily to her feet.

Snagging the edge of her heel on her chair, she stumbled.

Prince Reyes caught her arm. She gasped at the electricity sizzling over her skin. When she straightened, he dropped his arm and just stared at her.

A block of silence fell between them. For the life of her, Jasmine couldn't form any words to ease the sudden tension. Heat crawled over her body and her dress felt suddenly very restrictive.

Josh cleared his throat a third time, glanced from one to the other, then put his glass down. 'I need to find a business acquaintance. Please excuse me, Your Highness.' He bowed quickly, then scurried away before Jasmine could draw breath.

And once again, Jasmine was trapped by a pair of compelling grey eyes.

'Are you here with him?' Prince Reyes asked.

Did she detect a hint of disapproval in his tone? She raised her chin. 'No, I'm here on my own.'

If anything, his disapproval increased.

She scrambled to continue. 'I was told Rio was safe. So far nothing's happened to make me think otherwise.'

A gleam smouldered in his eyes. 'Danger comes in all forms, Miss Nichols. Sometimes in least expected packages. I'd urge you to practise caution.'

Hearing him use her surname instead of her first name as he had on the terrace, made her realise how much she missed hearing it.

'Thank you for the advice…umm…Your Highness.' She didn't add that she wouldn't need it. She didn't plan on being here long enough to get into any more danger than she was putting herself in tonight. In fact, as soon as she'd completed the hateful task, she was heading to the airport to catch the next flight out. 'But it's really not necessary.'

He continued to regard her in that disquieting manner. A

tiny shiver shimmied along her skin; the enormity of her task hit her, sharp and forceful.

Again the instinct to *run* slammed through her and it took everything Jasmine possessed to stand her ground and continue to meet his eyes.

This man possessed her only means to save her stepfather. Instead of dismissing his concern, she should be using it. The shame welling inside her didn't matter. The fear of stepping over the line couldn't be allowed to overtake the most important thing—saving Stephen. Saving her family.

She watched, scrambling to keep her distressing thoughts from showing, as Prince Reyes held out his hand. 'Very well. Far be it from me to cause offence by suggesting one of my bodyguards accompany you to your hotel. It was a pleasure to meet you, Miss Nichols.' He turned away and she noticed said bodyguards take their protective stance behind him. One was carrying the briefcase containing the treaty.

He was leaving! Taking with him the only chance of saving her stepfather.

Gripping her purse, she cleared her throat and quickly backpedalled. 'Actually, you're right. A strange city isn't a place for a woman to be wandering at night. I'd be grateful for your assistance.'

She heard the indrawn breath of the nearest guests, but ignored it.

Letting Prince Reyes leave was unthinkable. She'd travelled thousands of miles to make sure her stepfather didn't go to jail. Ten minutes was all she needed. Less, if she was really quick. She *had* to get her hands on that treaty. Even if it meant following a predator straight into his den.

He turned. Jasmine's breath stalled as his eyes darkened. He stared at her for what felt like an eternity before his lids descended. She sensed his withdrawal before he spoke.

'I'll arrange for my chauffeur to deliver you to your hotel.' He was already nodding to a dark-clad figure nearby.

Acute anxiety swelled inside her.

She couldn't fail. She just couldn't. Stephen might *just* survive prison but her mother wouldn't make it.

'Or I could come with you. Save your chauffeur making two trips,' she offered, cringing at the breathless tone of her voice.

He held up a hand to stop the bodyguard who stepped forward, his gaze imprisoning hers. Silence pulsed between them. A silence filled with charged signals that made the blood pulse heavily between her thighs. Every sense sprang into superawareness. She could hear every sound, smell every scent on the evening breeze, feel every whisper of air over her heating skin. Her nipples hardened and her cheeks heated at the blatant evidence of her awareness of him.

The thought that she was insanely attracted to a man whom she planned to deceive, albeit temporarily, caused hysterical laughter to bubble up.

She strained not to react. To keep the wrap draped over her arms and not use it to hide the proof of her arousal. She'd never used her feminine wiles to capture a man's attention. Doing so now made her insides clench with disgust. All the same, a small part of her gave a cry of triumph when his eyes dropped to her chest for an infinitesimal moment.

'You want to come with me? Now?' His voice had altered, his eyes narrowing with icy suspicion that warned her to tread carefully.

Jasmine couldn't afford to back away. She had too much to lose.

'Yes. Take me with you. My hotel isn't that far from here. I'll even buy you a drink as a thank you.' The single brain cell that remained shook with astonishment at her boldness. Afraid that her plea had emerged more of a command, and might perhaps cause offence, she hastily added, 'If you don't mind.'

His gaze darkened with a predatory gleam that made Jasmine swallow in trepidation. 'Perhaps it is you who should mind, Miss Nichols. Some would advise you against what you're asking.'

With deliberate slowness, she passed the tip of her tongue

over her lower lip. Stark hunger blazed in his eyes, stealing her breath as the grey depths turned almost black. A warm rush of air whispered over her skin, but even that small change caused her to gasp as if he'd physically laid his hands on her.

'Maybe, but something tells me I can trust you,' she replied, her nerves jangling with terror at the uncharted waters she found herself in. Flirting and sexual games had never been her forte. Not since her one attempt at university had ended in humiliating disaster.

Another step brought Prince Reyes within touching distance. His narrowed eyes, still holding that trace of sadness she'd glimpsed earlier, were now laced with a healthy dose of bitterness.

Jasmine didn't have time to dwell on his expression because his scent engulfed her, fuelling her already frenzied senses. She inhaled, filling her entire being with his essence. As if he sensed it too, his nostrils flared.

'You're playing a dangerous game, Jasmine,' he murmured.

'It…it's just a lift back to my h-hotel,' she croaked.

'Perhaps. Or it is something else. Something neither of us is ready for.' His voice was pitched low, for her ears alone. His gaze slid over her face, its path as forceful and yet as gentle as a silky caress.

'I'll be out of your hair in less than half an hour. Seriously, you have nothing to fear from me.' *Liar.* She tried to curb the accusing voice, thankful when it faded away under the onslaught of the heavy emotion beating in her chest.

His jaw tightened. 'I have everything to fear from you.' Again the bitterness, sharper this time. 'The curse of a beautiful woman has been my ancestors' downfall.'

She forced a laugh. *Beautiful? Her?* Well, if he could flatter, so could she. 'So prove it's not true. Deliver me to my hotel and walk away. Then you'll be free of this…curse.'

He tilted his head to one side, as if weighing her request. His hand rose again, this time to reach down to encircle her wrist.

With a subtle but firm tug, he pulled her to him.

'If walking away resolved centuries-old issues, my kingdom wouldn't be in shambles.'

'I didn't mean—'

He pulled her closer. Jasmine was too mesmerised by this enigmatic man to acknowledge the curious stares of the guests beyond the protective circle of Prince Reyes's bodyguards. And he didn't seem too disturbed by their growing audience.

His stare turned into a frown. 'You intrigue me, Jasmine Nichols.'

'Is that a bad thing?'

He stepped back and he seemed to come to a decision. 'I'm not certain, but I wish to find out. Come.'

Reyes Navarre drew a deep breath.

What in *Dios's* name was he doing? Not since Anaïs had he behaved so rashly. His carefree period of picking up liaisons for a night had come to a jagged halt five years ago when he'd experienced for himself just how duplicitous women could be. His own mother had hammered that lesson home forcefully in the weeks before her death.

Overnight, Reyes had witnessed the family he'd foolishly thought he could bring together disintegrate beyond recognition. He'd watched the will to live slowly extinguish from his father's eyes until only a husk remained.

Reyes's chest tightened painfully with equal parts of remorse and bitterness. Remorse that grew each day because he knew he'd failed to grant his father, King Carlos, his one wish—an heir to the throne while he was still alive. Bitterness because his father had condemned Reyes for choosing to learn from past mistakes. What his father didn't know was the woman Reyes had thought would be his queen had turned out to be just as conniving and as faithless as his own mother.

The double blow had made abstinence a far better prospect. One he'd embraced and pushed to the back of his mind when his father's health had worsened.

But tonight…

He glanced at the woman whose delicate scent filled every corner of the limo.

She hadn't spoken since they'd driven away from the banquet, but Reyes had caught the fleeting glances she sent his way every now and then. Just as he'd glimpsed the little darts of her tongue at the corner of mouth when her gaze fell on him.

She did it again, just then. A different sort of tightening seized his body.

Grinding his teeth, Reyes forced himself to examine why Jasmine Nichols intrigued him. Perhaps it was being away from Santo Sierra for the first time in over a year. Perhaps it was the knowledge that, after months of tough negotiations, Mendez had finally agreed to sign the trade treaty.

Or it could be that he just needed to let himself feel something other than bitterness and recrimination…to experience a moment of oblivion before the relentless pressure of his birthright settled back on his shoulders.

Whatever the reason, he didn't stop himself from pressing the intercom that connected him to the driver.

'Take us to the boat,' he instructed.

Jasmine immediately turned to him. 'You're not taking me to my hotel?' Her voice held a touch of trepidation but no hint of panic.

She knew the score.

As he should.

Except he didn't.

He was acting out of character. Had been from the moment he saw her.

His smile felt strained. 'You owe me a drink, I believe. I'm choosing to take it *before* I have you delivered to your hotel, not after.'

'Just in case I renege? You're not very trusting, are you?'

The twinge in his chest stung deeper, but he refused to acknowledge it. 'No, I'm not.'

Her eyes widened and she looked away. 'Are we really going to your boat?' she asked with a curious note in her voice.

'Yes.'

Reyes remembered she didn't like boats. Was that why he'd brought her to his yacht instead of the royal suite that awaited him at the Four Seasons? Was he hoping she would quail at the sight of the big floating palace and ask to be returned to her hotel?

Or had he brought her here for his own selfish reasons? Because, for some reason, focusing on her made his tumultuous feelings subside just a little?

All through the interminable dinner, he'd watched her, his gaze unable to stray from her for more than a few seconds because every time it had, he'd felt the darkness encroaching.

He watched her now from the corner of his eye, waiting for a reaction. But her hands remained folded in her lap, her gaze on the large vessel they'd pulled up to.

Unfortunately his thoughts and emotions suffered no such languor or calm. They churned in rhythm to the heavy pounding of his heart at what was to come.

Thoughts of sating himself on a woman had been pushed far back into the recesses of his mind, especially in the last year as he'd battled to salvage the trade treaty with Valderra. But his efforts had paid off.

He'd brought Mendez and Valderra to the treaty table, the result of which would mean a much-needed economic boost for his people.

Tomorrow they would complete the signing of the Santo-Valderra treaty. The concessions had been heavy. Mendez had made outrageous demands, like the excessively extravagant banquet held here tonight to honour his birthday. A ceremony Reyes had initially balked at attending, but had eventually given in to, because he suspected Mendez would use any excuse to postpone the final signing of the treaty.

The concessions Santo Sierra had given would be recouped with time. And, most importantly, the trade blockage had been removed.

He still faced an uphill battle in convincing his council

members to accept the changes to come. And there was also his father…

Reyes pushed thoughts of his father and grief aside and reminded himself that his father was alive.

And for one night, *this night*, Reyes intended to turn his mind to more…pleasant matters.

Jasmine sat in silence beside him, a beacon in the gloom that threatened to swallow him whole. But Reyes sensed that she was almost as reluctant as he to test the depths of awareness that zinged between them, just as he was quietly amazed by the depth of his attraction for her.

The memory of her skin when he'd held her on the balcony returned. His hand tightened next to his thigh.

He'd taken one look at Jasmine and the foundations of his self-imposed celibacy had started to shake. All through the banquet he'd been unable to take his eyes off her, a notion that had at once fascinated and irritated him. By the time the banquet was over, he'd known his resistance was severely compromised.

Yet, he'd been determined to walk away. Bitter experience and the heavy burden of duty had taught him to weigh his decisions carefully.

One-night stands weren't his *modus operandi*.

So what in the name of Dios *was he doing?*

He hadn't touched her since that last electrifying contact, and yet a storm unlike anything he'd ever known raged inside him. From the corner of his eye, he watched her fiddle with one earring. The sweet, yet provocative movement fanned the inferno of his lust.

'Are we going to get out?' Her question emerged with that same breathy, husky quality that sent shivers racing through him. Her eyes, blue like the ocean surrounding his kingdom, slid to his and the throb in his groin accelerated.

'Momentarily,' he replied, hoping for some last-minute perspective.

But the only perspective his brain was willing to consider

was the one where this enthralling woman ended up in his bed, her voluptuous body quenching his ferocious need.

She'd shown herself a worthy opponent, and yes, he considered the insane tug and pull of attraction between them a battleground. A battle from which he would emerge the victor and walk away with everything he held dear intact.

During their intriguing exchange not once had her gaze slid from his. In fact, more than once he'd seen a spark of defiance in the blue vividness of her eyes. That spark had ignited something inside him he'd long forgotten.

It had reminded him of a carefree time when life had been less fraught.

He glanced up at the lights of his yacht. He'd deliberately not moored at the same quay as Prince Mendez because he'd wanted to avoid the avid media attention Mendez courted.

Reyes preferred privacy…solitude…silence. His mother had created enough chaos in his life when she was alive.

So what are you doing bringing a total stranger on board?

He faced Jasmine.

Her gaze immediately riveted to his and heat surged through his bloodstream. She gave a nervous smile and pulled her wrap tighter around her. He frowned at the protective gesture. The interior of the car wasn't cold, in fact the night air blowing gently through the half-open windows was sultry. So there could be only one other reason for the telling gesture.

'It's not too late to change your mind.' His statement emerged harsher than he'd intended, partly, he realised, because he didn't want her to leave.

Her eyes widened and she wavered for a second before a curiously resolute look settled over her face. 'No. A deal is a deal. Although I'm not sure how to go about buying you a drink when we're boarding *your* boat.'

Relief made him exhale unsteadily. He signalled to his bodyguard, who opened the door. Reyes handed him the briefcase holding the treaty and held out his hand to Jasmine. 'We'll continue our debate on board.'

She glanced from his hand to his yacht. He held his breath. Slowly, she reached out. His grip tightened on her fingers as he stepped out of the car and helped her out. He'd taken two steps when he felt her tug at his grip.

'Wait. I can't do this.'

Disappointment curled through him. Reyes bit back a sharp retort as he dropped her hand. In the time since his last liaison, the world hadn't changed, then, he mused caustically. Women continued to tease, to engage in sexual games in the hope that playing hard to get would make them seem more attractive to the opposite sex. The bitterness he'd tried to douse welled up again.

'Save the excuses, Miss Nichols. I'm disappointed that women seem to believe creating intrigue involves mind games, but I am not willing to indulge you.' He nodded to his driver, who stepped forward. 'You'll be delivered to your hotel. Enjoy the rest of your stay in Rio.' He couldn't stem the regret that settled gut-deep inside him. Not to mention the uncomfortable arousal that tightened his groin and made thinking straight difficult.

He turned away, wanting to be far away from her, from the temptation of her voluptuous body and seductive scent that insisted on lingering in the air around him.

'Actually, that's not what I want.' She sounded hurt and a little confused. 'I didn't mean that I'd changed my mind about the drink.'

He whirled round. 'Then what did you mean, Jasmine?'

An uneasy look crossed her face. 'I told you, I don't really like boats. But I thought I'd make an exception...just this once...' She shook her head. 'Anyway, I'm not coming aboard wearing these shoes.' She gestured to her feet.

Puzzled, he frowned. 'What?'

'My step—umm, I read somewhere that heels and boats aren't a good combination.' Her shrug drew his attention to the silky curve of her shoulder. 'Of course, I don't know what sort of flooring you have on your yacht, but I don't want to ruin it.'

Laughter replaced Reyes's disappointment. It rumbled through his chest, a sensation he hadn't felt for a while.

'*My floors?* You don't want to ruin the floors on my boat?' His incredulity grew with his words and he barely stopped himself from shaking his head.

'No, I don't. Plus, my feet are seriously killing me. So if you don't mind?' She held out her hand for him to take. 'It'll only take a minute.'

Caught in the surreal moment, Reyes took her hand. He felt the rough ridge of scarred tissue and looked at the thin line crossing her palm. About to ask what had caused it, he was stalled by the sight of one graceful leg, lifted, one ankle strap unbuckled before the process was repeated with the other shoe.

His gaze dropped to her feet. They were small but perfectly formed with pink tips. The sight only aroused him further, tweaked his already dangerously heightened senses.

'Good idea,' he murmured inanely, his voice curiously hoarse.

She nodded and fell into step beside him. 'I think it's only fair to warn you, though, the last time I rode a dinghy, I ended up falling overboard. I hope you'll rescue me if that happens again?'

A smile tugged at his lips. 'As you can see, my boat is slightly bigger than your dinghy. It'll take a lot of effort to accidentally go overboard. But be assured, I'll come to your aid should the worst happen.'

'Well, if you put it that way, then I have nothing to worry about,' she said with a smile.

Reyes smiled, feeling less burdened than he had in a long time. He took her shoes as they approached the gangplank and followed her up the stairs onto the deck and through into the large, open salon. He watched her take in her surroundings, her mouth parting to inhale sharply at the opulence that embraced her.

Reyes had seen different reactions to his yacht, some openly covetous and some hidden behind careful indifference. Jasmine's eyes widened in something close to childlike, uninhibited awe as she took in the polished wood panels, gold ornamentation and monogrammed accessories in royal Santo Sierran blue he'd commissioned for the vessel.

'Wow!' She turned full circle and found him watching her. A faint blush touched her cheeks and she walked over to the large sofa and perched on the edge. 'Sorry, I didn't mean to gush.'

'A genuine reaction is better than artificial indifference.' He walked over to her and placed her shoes next to her.

'Seriously? Who would be indifferent to this?' She waved her hand around the deck.

'People with ulterior motives they prefer to hide?' The last female on this boat had been Anaïs. She'd been in full playing-hard-to-get mode, which had swiftly crumbled when Reyes had threatened to walk away. Of course, she'd had other aces up her sleeve. 'In my experience, people are rarely what they seem at first blush.'

'Oh, right.' Jasmine's eyes darted to his and slid away, and she seemed lost for words. Her tongue darted out to lick the corner of her lip.

Reyes's heart beat just that little bit faster. His fingers tightened as anticipation fizzed faster through his veins.

Her skin, creamy with the barest hint of tan, glowed under the soft lights of his deck. His fingers itched to touch, to caress. But he held back.

There would be time for that later. He had no doubt he was about to indulge in something he'd never indulged in before—a one-night stand; this could be nothing more than that—but he didn't want to rush it.

Morning would come soon enough. The treaty would be signed. He would ensure Santo Sierra's continued economic prosperity. And he would return to his father's bedside to continue his vigil.

But for now... 'I think it's time for that drink, yes?'

* * *

Jasmine swallowed her relief as the heated look in Prince Reyes's eyes abated. For a moment there, he'd looked as if he wanted to devour her where she stood.

And as much as that had sent a bolt of excitement through her, part of her had quailed at the look.

Hastily, she nodded. 'Yes, thank you.'

She watched him walk towards an extensive, gleaming wood-panelled bar. A steward approached, but he waved him away. Opening a chiller, he grabbed a bottle of wine and expertly uncorked it. Rounding the bar, he handed her a glass and indicated a row of low, luxurious sofas.

Taking the seat next to her, he lowered his long body into it, driving the breath straight out of her lungs.

'What shall we drink to?' he asked in a low, deep voice, his stare focused solely on her.

Jasmine's mouth dried. 'Um, how about congratulations on the progress you've made with the treaty so far?' Talking about the treaty helped keep her grounded, reminded her why she was here.

His smile held more than a hint of pride. *'Gracias.'*

'Did you achieve what you set out for?'

Against his usual guarded judgement he found himself sharing with her. 'It was a long, hard battle, but we're almost there. By this time tomorrow, a solid trade agreement will exist between our two kingdoms, something my people have needed for a long time.'

Jasmine's heart thudded loudly in her ears. Her hands started to shake and she hastily put her glass down. Sensing him following the movement, she flexed her fingers and smoothed them over her dress.

'You should be back there, then, at the museum, celebrating. Why did you leave early?'

'I don't like crowds,' he declared. His eyes widened, as if he'd let something slip he hadn't meant to. A moment later, his expression shuttered.

Something inside her softened. 'I don't like crowds, either.'

His head snapped up, his gaze searching hers. At her small smile, his tense jaw relaxed.

'I mean, who does, aside from rock stars and, well, crowd lovers?' she joked. She wasn't making much sense, but at the moment Jasmine would've kept babbling just to keep that smile on his face.

A small, enigmatic smile twitched his lips before he took a sip of his wine. 'So what brings you to Rio alone?' he asked. 'Carnival was last month.'

She forced herself not to tense. For a wild moment Jasmine wondered if he could see through her to the truth of her presence in his life.

Clearing her throat, she shrugged and struck for the half-truth she'd practised in her head. 'I haven't had a holiday in years. An unexpected gap opened up in my schedule, and I took it.'

His eyes slowly narrowed, his fingers stilling around his wine glass. 'And you just happened to gain the most sought-after invitation to the Prince of Valderra's birthday party?' Mild disbelief rang through his voice.

'No. Of course not. My trip isn't all play. The brokerage firm I work for have been following the Santo-Valderra negotiations for some time. When one of my...clients offered me the invitation, I thought it would be good experience to learn more about it.'

'And have you?'

Jasmine shook her head. 'Only what's been released to the press, which is plenty interesting. I mean, from a brokerage point of view, it's mind-blowing what you've achieved—'

Jaw tightening, he set his glass down with a sharp click. 'And you want to know more? To gain first-hand information? Is that why you're here?'

CHAPTER THREE

JASMINE SWALLOWED, TREPIDATION jangling her nerves. 'I am interested, yes. But no, it's not why I'm here.' She spoke through the shame-coated lie.

His gaze dropped to her mouth. Heat rose in her belly, slowly engulfing her chest, her throat.

She fought to breathe as the feral, dangerously hungry look once more stole over his face, permeating the air with thick, saturated lust.

He reached out a hand, caught a lock of hair in his fingers and slowly caressed it. 'Why exactly are you here, Jasmine Nichols? Why did you not demand to be returned to your hotel?'

'I meant what I said. I'm intrigued by the treaty.' That much was true. 'From what I've been able to learn about it—'

He frowned. 'What you've been able to learn? Are you a spy?'

'No!' she replied hurriedly. Hoping she wasn't digging herself into an even deeper hole, she continued. 'The firm I work for brokers deals like these all the time, on a much smaller scale…and I was just wondering if what I'd heard was right.'

'What did you hear?'

'That the treaty heavily favours Valderra…' Her voice drifted away as a dark look blanketed his face.

God, what was she doing?

She wouldn't be surprised if he threw her off the boat for prying.

'Concessions were made prior to my handling of the negotiations that I have no choice but to honour.' He didn't sound happy about it. Just resigned.

She nodded. His fingers grazed her cheek. She only had to

turn her head a fraction and she'd feel more of his touch. Her every sense craved that touch.

He drew closer, slowly, his fingers winding around a lock of her hair; his eyes not leaving hers. 'Why do I get the feeling that you're holding something back from me, Jasmine?' he asked again, softly this time, his breath fanning over her lips. 'Tell me why I'm fighting my instincts when I should be heeding them?'

Her insides quaked with fear…and anticipation. 'I guess I could tell you that you're not the only one feeling that way. There's something about you. Something overpowering, that makes me…'

'Makes you what?'

Shaking her head, she surged to her feet and stumbled to the railing. Frustrated tears stung her eyes as she stared into the dark waters.

She couldn't do this.

She'd come too far, clawed herself back from a destructive, chaotic past. Going through with Joaquin's plan, giving in to the thug's demands would mean stepping back into that dark tunnel.

But walking away meant Stephen's destruction. A broken mother.

She gulped down the sob that threatened.

And jumped when his lips touched the back of her neck. A mere graze. But it pushed back her dark despair, lit her up like a bonfire on a sultry summer's night. As if galvanised by that simple touch, she came alive.

He grabbed her to him, one hand sliding around her shoulder while the other gripped her waist. He kissed the delicate skin below her ear, imprinting himself on her so vividly, every atom in her body screeched in delight.

He spun her in his arms and kissed her.

Jasmine had been kissed before. But not like this. Never like this. The fiery tingle started from her toes, spread through her body like wildfire, stinging her nerve endings. He tasted of wine, of dark, strong coffee, of heady pleasure that made her heart hammer as he drew her even closer.

Her breasts crushed into his chest. The imprint of his muscled torso against hers caused her fingers to tighten on his nape. He growled something under his breath, but the words were crushed between their lips as they both moved to deepen the kiss.

Somewhere deep within, a voice cautioned her against what she was doing. She tried to heed it, tried to pull back. Vaguely she sensed him move towards a doorway in the saloon.

Her good sense kicked in. 'Wait...'

He carried on walking, his lips now straying to the astonishingly sensitive skin just below her ear. She shuddered, a melting deep inside that threatened to drown her.

'Umm...' She paused as she realised she didn't know what to call him. What was the etiquette when you were snogging the face off a South American Crown Prince? 'Your Highness... wait...'

His deep laugh made her blush. 'When we are alone, you may call me Reyes. After all, you can hardly call me Your Highness when I'm deep inside you,' he murmured into her ear. 'Although that does present interesting possibilities...'

Her shocked gasp brought another laugh and Jasmine had to scramble to hang on to her sanity. 'Please...Reyes, put me down,' she pleaded.

Sensing her agitation, he slowly lowered her down before capturing her hands in his. 'What is it, Jasmine?'

For one absurd moment, she wanted to blurt out her guilt, but bit her tongue at the last minute. 'I haven't...I mean, this isn't something I normally do,' she babbled instead.

Raising both her hands, he pressed kisses onto her knuckles, his stunning eyes cooling. 'I understand. This is where you establish ground rules? Where I let you name your price because I'm too lust-hazed to see straight?' he asked cynically.

The ground rocked beneath her. Somewhere along the line, life had dealt this man serious blows. The depths of his sadness, suspicion and cynicism weren't traits he'd picked up by chance. And she should know. Life could be cruel beyond measure. Especially with men like Joaquin calling the shots.

But they only win if you let them...

The rebellious teenager whose antics had landed her in juvenile detention threatened to break through. Reminding herself just what was at stake here, she swallowed. 'Is it too much to believe that I'm nervous and a little bit overwhelmed?'

He lowered her hands. His eyes narrowed, probed and assessed. Jasmine understood how it was that Reyes Navarre had negotiated the sometimes almost insurmountable treaty with Valderra.

'So you don't want anything from me?' he asked.

Only the gritty determination that had seen her stand up to dangerous men twice her size kept her gaze from falling. 'Honestly, I would like to see the treaty. But I won't be sleeping with you because of that...' She realised what she was saying and stopped. A scalding blush suffused her face. 'I mean, nothing happens here that won't be my choice—'

He stopped her with a finger to her mouth.

'Understood. But remember this, too. Whatever happens between us will not go beyond tonight. It cannot,' he stated imperiously. 'My desire for you is finite.'

Hearing the words so starkly drew a cold shiver from her in spite of passion's flames arcing between them. He felt it and immediately captured her shoulders. 'But make no mistake. This desire burns bright and strong and I promise to make the experience—should you *choose* to stay for it—pleasurable for you.'

His accent had thickened, his words burning away the cold as if it had never existed. He lowered his head and brushed his lips over hers.

Jasmine swallowed as his words echoed in her head. A powerful aphrodisiac intent on eroding rational thought.

Walk away. Now!

She groaned and pulled away. 'I can't. I know you probably think I'm a tease, but I promise, I'm not. I'm not in the habit of jumping into bed with a man I just met. I hope you understand?'

Her mind made up, she took another step back and picked up her clutch. She couldn't go through with it. She would find another way to save her stepfather. Whatever the repercussions, Jasmine would find a way to help Stephen and her mother deal with it.

But not this.

Whatever Joaquin needed the copy of the treaty for no longer mattered to her. The man who stood in front of her, who'd battled whatever demons haunted him to achieve this treaty for his kingdom, didn't deserve what she'd planned tonight. *She* would never be able to live with herself if she went through with it; if she took a step back to that dark place she'd sworn never to revisit again.

Her heart lifted, lightened, filled with relief.

She looked up at Reyes and experienced a little thrill at the stark shock and disappointment on his face. She had reduced a powerful, virile man to…what had he called himself before? Lust-crazed?

Slightly heady with the feeling, she took another stumbling step back before she succumbed to temptation.

She was in an exotic country, in the presence of a charismatic man who seemed to set her very soul on fire. Jasmine knew that if she gave in—*and she wouldn't!*—the experience with Reyes would be unique and would remain with her for ever.

After several more moments staring at her, he finally nodded. 'Very well. I'll summon my driver.'

Acute loss scythed through her. 'That would be great, thank you.'

She watched him walk to the intercom next to the bar, holding her breath to keep from blurting for him to stop.

About to press the black button, he paused and looked over

at her. 'It's not every day that I'm surprised, but you've succeeded in pulling the rug from beneath my feet,' he said.

'Umm…thanks. But why are you surprised?'

That reserved smile made another appearance and he turned. 'You want me, but you're walking away. I may not know why, but I admire the strong principle behind your decision. Perhaps you deserve a prize after all.'

'Oh?' Renewed excitement fizzed beneath her skin.

He retraced his steps and held out his hand. 'If you still want to see it, I'll show you the treaty.'

Oh. Jasmine wanted to refuse. Wanted to demand another prize, one that involved his mouth on hers. But that opportunity had passed. She'd refused Prince Reyes. A man like that wouldn't place himself in a position to be spurned twice.

But neither could she resist the chance to glimpse a piece of Santo-Valderran history.

He led her down several flights of stairs into the heart of the yacht. Images of soft, mellow wood and rich chrome touched the edge of her consciousness. There seemed to be a lot of gold—chandeliers, paintings frames, doorknobs—but Jasmine was too caught up in Reyes Navarre's magnificence and the electric awareness where his hand held hers for details of the décor to register.

She finally regained her senses when he released her upon entering his study. The space was masculine, the furniture rich antique. Expensive books on diplomacy, economics and culture lined one wall. First-edition literary works lined the other. Behind his desk, a Renaissance painting that would've had museum curators salivating graced the wall.

He smiled at her and skirted his desk. He pressed a lever beneath the painting and it swung back to reveal a safe. He entered a code and pressed his thumb against a digital scanner.

Jasmine held her breath as he slid out an expensive leather folder and came to stand beside her. Very conscious of the breadth of his shoulders and the heat emanating from his whipcord body, she struggled to focus on the treaty.

When the terms finally registered, she frowned. 'Why would you agree to this?'

'The terms aren't up for discussion. I need to make the best of this situation.'

Puzzled, she stared at him. His gaze captured hers before dropping to her mouth. Awareness crackled through the air. Sucking in a breath, she refocused on reading the final pages. She noticed that various preliminary terms had been agreed every year for the past three years, the first signed by his father. Prince Mendez had played a cunning game, increasing his demands with each passing year.

She started to turn the last page. Reyes put his hand over hers. 'The remaining terms are confidential.'

The effect of his hand on hers again made her pulse jump. 'And what? You don't trust me?' she joked, hoping to inject a little lightness to ease the thick tension filling the room.

His hand trailed up her arm to slide around her nape. Tilting her head, he looked deep into her eyes. 'Trust doesn't come easy to me, but I've trusted you with more tonight than I have anyone in a long time, Jasmine.'

Her breath squeezed through the lump clogging her throat. 'Why?'

He shrugged. 'Perhaps I'm learning to trust my instincts again. Perhaps because you're the only one who didn't enjoy Mendez's antics earlier.' He smiled again.

Despite his attempt at a joke, Jasmine remained fiercely glad of her decision not to give in to Joaquin's threat; she blinked back hot tears and smiled. 'You have no idea how much that means to me.'

The lightness evaporated. He stepped closer, an almost desperate hunger screaming from his body. 'I still want you, Jasmine. Very badly.'

Throwing caution to the wind shouldn't have come so easily, shouldn't have felt so freeing. Because she'd learned very early that everything came at a cost.

But she replied, 'Take me,' before she registered the enormity of the plunge she was taking.

The sensation of luxurious covers beneath her back was the first inkling that they'd left his study. The equally luxurious feel of him as he lowered himself on top of her confirmed that thought.

Crushed by his delicious weight, she couldn't mistake the imprint of his impressive arousal pushing against her. Hot sensation pierced her, settling low in her belly as he deepened the kiss. His tongue delved into her mouth, commencing a bold exploration that left her reeling and struggling to hold on to the last of her sanity.

His hands slid down her sides, creating a path of heat wherever he touched. Locating her side zip, he eased it down.

At the touch of fingers on her skin, Jasmine gasped.

He raised his head, his dark grey eyes spiking into hers. 'Your skin is so soft, so silky,' he murmured huskily.

'Thank you,' she responded, then cringed, feeling suddenly gauche and awkward. The first time she'd done this, it had ended badly. *Beyond badly.* The second time had been worse. What if third time *wasn't* lucky…?

She lost her train of thought as he gripped her hip. His heat penetrated the silk material to her skin, fanning the flame already building inside her. Wanting to experience even more of his warmth, she raised her head and traced his mouth with her tongue.

Her action drew a gasp from him, his eyes darkening even further as heat scoured over his taut cheekbones. 'I hope you'll forgive me,' he murmured distractedly as he nuzzled her jaw, planting feverish kisses that caused her heart to pound harder.

'What for?' she managed to squeeze out.

He settled firmer against her. 'It's been a while for me. I will want to take my time.'

A wave of heat engulfed her face. 'Oh. Yes…well, it's been a while for me, too.'

A look crossed his face, almost of relief. Jasmine's heart

swelled, her hand finally unclasping itself from his neck to caress his cheek. He planted an open-mouthed kiss in her palm. That intimate caress drew another gasp from her. Pleased by her reaction, he traced his mouth over her wrist, down her arm to the curve of her elbow, and licked the pulse.

Fire erupted in her pelvis so fierce and sweet, she moaned.

Galvanised by her response, he levered himself off her and stood beside the bed.

Jasmine had never imagined watching a man undress would trigger anything but embarrassment. But watching Reyes shed his clothes became another heady experience. Enthralled, she watched him ease his tuxedo jacket off his broad shoulders before releasing the studs of his shirt. Her mouth watered as his deeply bronzed chest was revealed. Her fingers itched to touch, to explore. Curling them into the covers, she held still and adored his beauty with her eyes.

'The look in your eyes threatens to unman me, *querida*,' he rasped. His fingers went to the button on his trousers.

Embarrassed that she'd done something wrong, Jasmine started to look away.

'No. Don't look away,' he commanded.

Her eyes flew to his. 'But you said—'

'*Sí*, I know, but I hate the thought of being deprived of your attention.' With an impatient shove, he kicked the rest of his clothes away and stood before her, gloriously, powerfully naked.

Jasmine silently thanked him for giving her permission to look. Because she couldn't have looked away now if her life depended on it.

He was spectacular! He stepped closer and she watched, fascinated, as the clearly delineated muscles moved beneath his skin.

Her stomach clenched with renewed arousal when he reclined next to her. 'I want you naked.'

She wanted to find fault with his imperious tone, but Jasmine would've been a hypocrite if she didn't acknowledge that every word that fell from his lips only further increased her excitement. Lending action to his words, he brushed aside her hair, slid one hand under her dress's thin strap and eased it off her shoulder.

He feasted his eyes on her, scouring every inch of her breasts as if committing them to memory. With a firm tug on her bra, he bared one nipple, a guttural groan rumbling from his chest as he lowered his head and sucked her flesh into his mouth. He teased, he tormented. His fingers traced, paused over a scar on her shoulder, a remnant from her shady past.

She held her breath, her fingers convulsed in his hair, holding him to his task even as she tensed in anticipation of a query. His touch moved on. When he turned his attention to her other breast, Jasmine whimpered in delight and relief.

Dazed, she felt him tug her dress off. Her panties and bra followed, discarded by urgent hands that caressed her skin with masterful strokes.

Wet heat pooled between her legs, a fact Reyes's exploratory fingers didn't miss when one possessive hand cupped her feminine core.

Raising his head from her tight, wet nipple, he speared her with a fiery gaze. 'Maybe I won't go slow after all. I have to have you now,' he rasped.

The next few seconds whizzed by in a blur, the sound of the condom wrapper tearing open barely impinging on her heated senses. He gathered her to him before she could draw breath. Placing himself between her thighs, he speared his hands in her hair and angled her face to his.

Eyes the colour of gunmetal held her prisoner.

He thrust inside her fast, hard, then immediately set a blistering pace that stripped her of every thought.

Their coupling was furious. Heady in ways she'd never dreamed sex could be. She screamed as the first, fierce climax hit her. He kissed away her shocked cries, almost greedy in his possession of her mouth, then slowed his pace just long enough for her spasms to ease.

Then he surged to his knees, placed her in front of him and entered her from behind. Guttural, indecipherable Spanish words spilled from him as he thrust over and over inside her, one strong arm clamped around her waist. Her throat clogged with emotion, her heart pounding wildly in her chest as tears gathered in her eyes at the magic she hadn't come looking for, but had miraculously found.

Reaching up behind her, she clasped his nape, turned her head and met his lips with hers. They stayed like that, their sweat-slicked bodies rocking back and forth until he tensed, a harsh groan rumbling through his chest, followed by convulsions that triggered her second, deeper orgasm.

His arm remained locked around her as he eased them back onto the bed, their harsh breaths gentling. He brushed away the damp hair from her face before placing a gentle kiss on her temple.

'This wasn't how I foresaw my evening ending when I arrived at the museum tonight.'

Jasmine tensed, the thought that he could be regretting what happened sending a vein of ice through her chest. Some otherworldly, more experienced woman would've found a sophisticated answer to his comment. But no such words rose to her mind, so she clamped her eyes shut and held her breath.

'Nor mine,' she murmured.

'You were amazing,' he muttered, his tone hushed.

The breath whooshed from her lungs, joy making her lips curve in a smile that seemed to emerge from her very heart. 'You weren't so bad, yourself.'

He laughed, a low, husky sound she'd begun to seriously like. With a kiss on her shoulder, he eased himself from her body and stood up.

'Come.' Again his tone was more command than request.

Again, Jasmine found she didn't mind. 'Where are we going?'

'I have a sudden need to see your body slick with water.'

He tugged her off the bed and led her into a luxurious

shower room. After adjusting various dials and testing the water with his fingers, he turned.

He dropped a kiss at the juncture between her neck and shoulder. With swift, efficient motions he secured her hair on top of her head.

Grasping her shoulders, he walked her into the misty cubicle and proceeded to wring every last ounce of pleasure from her body.

Afterwards, wrapped in a warm, fluffy towel, Jasmine watched Reyes, his lean, masculine body stealing her breath once again.

'I'm glad I met you tonight.' The words spilled out before she could stop them.

Their eyes connected, held. 'I feel the same,' he said simply. They both looked away at the same time.

In silence he led her back to his bed. And this time, their lovemaking was slow, languid, an unhurried union that brought an alien tightness to her chest and tears to her eyes. Before their heartbeats had slowed, Reyes had fallen asleep.

The low buzz of her phone woke her. Squinting in the dark, she saw the light from her smartphone illuminate the inside of her small clutch purse. The call could only be from England. And since her boss knew she was on holiday and was unlikely to disturb her, it could only be her parents...or Joaquin.

Her heart jumped into her throat.

Reyes had eased his tight hold of her during the night and now lay on his stomach, his head turned away from her.

Quickly, she slid out of bed and retrieved the phone. Seeing the name displayed on the screen, her heart plummeted. 'Hello.'

'Jasmine!' Her mother's frantic voice rang in her ears. 'Where are you? They took him. Oh, God, they broke his arm...and then they took him away!'

Walking on tiptoe to the door, Jasmine slipped out and hurried down the hallway to Reyes's study. 'Mum, take a deep breath and tell me what happened,' Jasmine said, even though deep down she suspected the answer.

'Some men broke into the house and they took Stephen!'

'*What?* When?'

'About an hour ago. They wouldn't say where they were going. But they hurt him, Jasmine. What if they...they kill him?' Her voice broke in a strangled sob.

Ice slithered down Jasmine's spine. She clutched the phone to her ear to stem the shaking in her hand. 'It's okay, Mum. I'm sure they won't. Did they...what did they say?' She tried to steady her voice so her mother's panic didn't escalate.

'They left a number...asked me to give it to you to call. Jasmine, I don't know what I'll do if anything happens to Stephen— *Oh, God!*'

Knowing how adversity had affected her mother before Stephen came into their lives, Jasmine clutched the phone harder, unwilling to contemplate the worst. Her earlier bravado began to wither before her eyes.

She took a deep breath. 'Well, stop worrying.' Jasmine tried to infuse as much optimism into her voice as she could. 'Text me the number. I'll sort this out, I promise.'

Her mother's teary, panic-laced goodbye wrenched at Jasmine's heart. Hands shaking, she started to dial the number her mother had sent through when her phone buzzed with another incoming text.

Jasmine read it. Once. Twice. Her fingers went numb.

The message itself was innocuous enough. But the meaning hit her square in the chest.

One hour. Rio Hilton. Room 419. A simple exchange. Good luck.

She returned to the bedroom on leaden feet and froze as Reyes shifted in the bed, exhaled heavily before settling back into deep sleep. Moonlight filtering through the open windows silhouetted him in soft light, his glorious body bare from the waist up. Momentarily, she stared, recalling the way he'd unleashed all that potent power on her, his generosity in showering her with pleasure.

Her insides quivered as harsh reality hit her in the face.

She had no choice.

She'd been willing to abort her despicable mission even if it meant exposing her stepfather's misdeeds and possible incarceration to the authorities.

But she couldn't stand by and do nothing while Stephen was being physically harmed. Or worse. She would never be able to live with herself.

As for Reyes...

She bit her lip and forced her gaze from the man lying on the bed.

Numbness invading every atom of her being, Jasmine stealthily pulled her clothes on and went back into the study. Reyes hadn't had the chance to place the treaty back in the safe.

Insides clenched in shame, she walked to the desk, opened the folder and lifted the heavily embossed papers.

Her hands shook as she lifted the treaty and held it in her hands.

'I am merely a concerned citizen of Santo Sierra, wishing to reassure myself my crown prince's actions are altruistic, Miss Nichols. That is all...'

Joaquin's words reverberated in her head and she clenched her teeth. She might only have known him for a few hours, but Jasmine didn't doubt that Crown Prince Reyes Navarre cared deeply about his people and held only their best interests at heart.

It was Joaquin's motives that were highly suspect.

Whatever happened, Jasmine didn't have any intention of letting the document out of her sight.

Taking a deep breath, she folded the treaty, slipped into the hallway and made her way to the deck to retrieve her shoes. Clutching them to her chest, she made her way down the steps towards the gangplank.

The bodyguard materialised in front of her, large and threatening. His searching eyes stalled her breath.

With every last ounce of strength, she straightened and lifted her chin, all at once ashamed and thankful that her old skills were coming to the fore.

Never show fear, never show fear. 'Can I get a taxi, please?' she asked, praying he spoke enough English to understand her request.

For several seconds, he didn't respond. Finally, he nodded and indicated the exit.

Despite the pre-dawn hour, people and cars rushed past on the road beyond the quay, the post-Carnival Rio nightlife as vibrant as it had been during the festival a month ago. Another set of bodyguards guarded the gangplank and exchanged words with her escort, who shrugged and said something that made the others chuckle. Jasmine tried to remain calm, regulate her breathing as she walked beside him.

Twenty minutes later, she stumbled into the foyer of the Rio Hilton. The night receptionist directed her to the bank of lifts without batting an eyelash.

When she reached the room, Joaquin Esteban's burly sidekick held the door open for her. She entered. The diminutive man rose from a cream-coloured sofa, his hands outstretched in false greeting. Jasmine sidestepped him, her fists clenched.

'What did you do with my stepfather?' she demanded.

Joaquin paused, his hard eyes glittering before his sleazy smile slid back into place. 'Why, nothing, Miss Nichols. He's fine and currently enjoying the best hospitality at my home in London until our business is concluded.'

'You broke his arm!'

'Ah, that was rather unfortunate. My men merely wanted to make sure everyone understood what moves needed to be made. But he got a little…excited.'

Rage built inside her. 'So you broke his arm? God, you're nothing but a thug!'

'I would caution against name-calling. You were on the

prince's yacht for over five hours. And from the looks of it you weren't there against your will.'

Her skin crawled. 'You were having me watched?'

'I'm very vested in our deal. It's imperative that you understand that.' His eyes slid from her face to her handbag, the question in them undeniable.

For a wild second, Jasmine wanted to tell him she'd failed.

She wanted to turn back the clock; to return the treaty, return to the bed and the magnificent, captivating man she'd left in it. A man whose haunted eyes made her yearn to comfort him.

Even now she craved one more look, one more touch...

But it was too late. Defying Joaquin would be condemning her stepfather to a horrific fate.

And yet, she couldn't just hand the document over.

'You're not merely a concerned citizen of Santo Sierra, are you?'

Joaquin shrugged. 'No. Valderra is my home.'

Her mouth dropped open in shock. What on earth had she got herself into? 'Why are you doing this?' she whispered. Just then another possibility dawned, cold and unwelcoming. 'Do you work for Prince Mendez?'

'Enough questions. The document, please,' Joaquin said coldly.

'No.' Jasmine shook her head and eyed the door. 'I won't give it to you.'

She whirled about and was confronted with the thick wall of muscle in the shape of the bodyguard. His beady eyes narrowed before he snatched the clutch out of her frozen grasp and removed the treaty from it.

Jasmine had been in enough fights to know which ones she stood a chance in and which ones were hopeless.

Joaquin's eyes glittered as he perused the sheets, before rolling up the document.

'Thank you, Miss Nichols. I think this concludes our business together.' He started to turn away.

Sick with self-loathing, she stepped forward. 'Wait! Please tell me you'll return the treaty to Prince Reyes before tomorrow?'

'You don't need to trouble yourself about that,' Joaquin answered. 'I'll make sure it reaches the right hands.'

Sweat coated her palms. 'But if the document isn't returned tonight, Rey…the prince will know I stole it.'

'And what does that matter? It's highly unlikely you and the prince will ever cross paths again, is it not? Besides, going on past experience, I wouldn't have imagined you would be bothered by something as trivial as your reputation,' he scoffed.

'I'm not that person any more. I've turned my life around.'

'So you say. But once a thief, always a thief. You reverted to type quite easily.'

Pain frayed the outer edges of her heart. Holding her head high, she stood her ground. 'I don't need to prove myself to you.' Anxiety churned through her stomach. 'What about Stephen?'

'He'll be home for breakfast. Goodbye, Miss Nichols.' He walked out of the room.

Jasmine wanted to chase after him, rip the document from his hands.

As if guessing her intentions, the bodyguard cleared his throat.

Jasmine didn't flinch. She'd dealt with brutes like him before, taken down one or two, even. But she knew she wouldn't win this battle. She'd been damned from the very start.

Nevertheless, the enormity of what she'd done settled like a heavy mantle on her shoulders. Ice flowed through her veins as she clenched her fists.

'Taxi?' the bodyguard snarled.

'No, thank you. I'll find my own way.'

The first rays of dawn slashed across the sky as Jasmine returned to her hotel. With disjointed movements, she wheeled her suitcase out of the closet and stuffed her belongings into it. Forcing herself not to think, not to feel, she undressed and entered the shower.

But tears, scalding hotter than the scouring spray, coursed down her cheeks as she desperately scrubbed her skin.

Tonight she'd sunk to a despicable low. She'd lied. She'd stolen.

She'd let herself down spectacularly.

And in the blink of an eye, stripped back the years and reverted to her old self.

CHAPTER FOUR

One month later

APRIL HAD BROUGHT an abrupt end to the cold snap and incessant rain that had engulfed London and most of the country for months.

Jasmine stepped out of Temple tube station into brilliant sunshine and stumbled past a group of tourists debating which attraction to visit. Their excited conversation barely touched her consciousness. Arms folded around her middle, she struck a path through the crowd towards the building that housed her office, clinging to the near fugue state she'd inhabited since returning from Rio. A blank mind meant she didn't have to think. Didn't have to feel.

Didn't have to remember Reyes.

Or what she'd done.

Most of all, she didn't have to acknowledge the fact that the past she'd thought she'd left behind was still with her, buried underneath her skin, ready to rear its ugly head and reveal itself in all its glory.

Naïve. She'd been so naïve. To imagine that she could escape unharmed.

A lance of pain shot through her chest. By now Reyes Navarre would know her for what she was. And despise her for it.

Despite the thousands of miles separating them, Jasmine could almost feel the weight of his disappointment.

'I've trusted you with more tonight than I have anyone in a long time.'

A moan rose in her throat. With a shake of her head, she ruthlessly suppressed it, sucking in a deep breath as she neared her office building.

Her boss had been sending her anxious looks over the past few days. Twice this week, she'd forgotten it was her turn to get the coffee and muffins.

Yesterday she'd returned from a hurried trip to the coffee shop with a serious case of nausea. One she hadn't been able to shake since.

Numbness and absent-mindedness when she was alone was fine...welcome in fact. But she couldn't afford to let it affect her work—

Her thoughts scattered as a body slammed into her.

Jasmine grasped the nearest solid thing to break her fall, but it was too late. She slid sideways, taking with her half of the contents of the small newsstand as she stumbled.

'For goodness' sake, miss, watch where you were going! Now look what you've done!'

Glaring at the retreating back of the man who'd barrelled into her, Jasmine regained her feet and started gathering the magazines. 'I'm so sorry,' she muttered.

'It'll take me ages to sort out the newspapers,' the kiosk owner grumbled.

'It's fine. I'll pay for—' Jasmine's words dried in her throat.

From the numbed state she'd lived in for the past four weeks, the fiery bolt of electricity that smashed through her body made her reel. Her heart thundered, sending a rush of blood roaring through her veins so she didn't hear the concerned voices around her as she grabbed the newspaper, her gaze riveted on the picture on the front page.

Reyes!

Her fingers shook, wildly fluttering the paper as she stared. Reyes...the reclusive crown prince...on the front page of an English newspaper. The why slammed into her brain a split second before her eyes sought the headlines.

Santo-Valderra Trade Treaty In Chaos... Economy Threatened!

An anguished moan scoured her throat, her heart lurching so painfully she had visions of it stopping altogether.

'Miss, are you all right?' the kiosk owner's voice finally impinged.

Trembling, she dug into her bag and paid for the newspaper, mumbling at the seller to keep the change to pay for the damage she'd caused.

Clutching the paper, she darted through the crowd, breaking into a full run as fevered urgency flooded her bloodstream.

In her office, she sank into her seat, her shaking fingers spreading open the newspaper.

She blinked eyes that stung, forced back her panic and focused on the words of the story.

The Santo-Valderra talks had broken down after Prince Reyes Navarre had been unable to produce his part of the treaty. Prince Mendez of Valderra had agreed to continue treaty talks on condition his further demands were met.

Mendez had walked away from the negotiation table when his demands had been refused. Now both kingdoms were at an economic stand-off.

Acid churned through her gut as she turned over the pages to find the rest of the story. But things only got worse.

Unable to keep the bile down, Jasmine stumbled from her desk and barely made the toilet before she emptied the meagre contents of her stomach.

Oh, God, this was all her fault!

Shakily, she returned to her desk, read the story one more time, and fished out her phone. The small part of her brain that could function sent a small prayer of thanks that her boss had left last night for an overseas assignment.

After sending a quick email taking the day off, she entered a search into her computer. Locating Santo Sierra's embassy in London, she jotted down the address, slipped it into her bag and left her office.

By the time the taxi delivered her outside the embassy in Kensington, her shaking had abated. Her insides still trembled, but outwardly she projected the picture of calm she'd strived so hard to achieve over the last few years.

Striding into the opulent reception, she made a beeline for the receptionist. Jasmine wasn't sure exactly what her game plan was, but she had to do *something*.

Maybe she could speak to the ambassador, convince someone to let her try to fix the chaos she'd created...

God, she was grasping at straws. But she couldn't cower away—

'Can I help you?'

She focused on the receptionist. 'Yes.' She stopped and cleared her throat. 'Can I see the ambassador, please?'

The receptionist's eyebrows rose. 'Do you have an appointment?'

'No...but I...this is important...' Jasmine ventured, her voice trailing off when the neatly dressed woman shook her head.

'Perhaps you'd like to leave your name and the reason for your visit and I'll arrange an appointment...?'

Jasmine smothered a grimace. 'My name is Jasmine Nichols. And it's about the Santo-Valderra treaty.'

The other woman's eyes narrowed suspiciously. 'What about it?'

'I just read in the paper about it breaking down. I wanted to offer my help in any way I can...?'

The receptionist stared at her in silence, her scepticism turning to downright incredulity as the seconds ticked by. The phone rang. She picked it up. The conversation in rapid Spanish flew over Jasmine's head.

She focused when the receptionist gasped. *'Sí. Sí. Su Alteza.'*

Her eyes widened as she replaced the handset. 'Please take a seat, Miss Nichols. Someone will be with you shortly.'

The flood of relief that surged through Jasmine nearly crippled her. Reaching out, she gripped the edge of the desk. 'Oh, thank you. I know he's busy, but I really appreciate it.' She started to walk towards the plush seats, then froze when her stomach heaved.

Swallowing, she turned. 'Can I use your bathroom?' she asked, alarm rising when her stomach roiled harder.

The receptionist was still staring at her as if she'd grown extra limbs, but Jasmine was too desperate not to heave onto the polished floor to decipher why. Eyes wide, the other woman pointed down a small hallway. 'Through those doors.'

Nodding, she rushed into the bathroom and locked the stall. Five minutes of wretched heaving later, she stared at her reflection in the mirror and groaned.

How did she expect anyone to take her seriously when she looked like an electrified corpse? She dampened another roll of hand tissues and pressed them to her cheeks. Whatever was ailing her would have to be investigated later.

Drying her hands, she pinned a confident smile on her face, exited the bathroom. And came face to face with Prince Reyes Navarre.

The pounding in Reyes's head when he'd learned that Jasmine Nichols was in his embassy had subsided to a dull throb.

For a single moment his rage had been total. All-encompassing. The feeling had been followed closely by shock at her sheer audacity.

It'd been several moments before he'd realised the ambassador was about to turn her away. His countermand had raised several eyebrows around the conference table where he'd been conducting his meeting. He hadn't explained his reason.

He didn't need to.

His plan for retribution where Jasmine Nichols's betrayal was concerned was no one's business but his.

He watched with satisfaction as she paled. That prim little smile on her face disappeared and her eyes rounded.

'Reye—Prince Navarre!'

Was that a tremble of fear? Good.

'You will address the prince as Your Highness.' His ambassador spoke sharply from beside him.

Jasmine's gaze swung from him to the short, fatherly figure, and back to him. Noting for the first time that they had an audience, she blinked. Reyes noted her drawn features.

If she had a conscience, he hoped it was eating away at her. But he knew women like her possessed no conscience. They seduced and betrayed with no thought for anyone else but themselves.

His jaw tightened as her lashes swept down in a false gesture of apology.

'Of course. My apologies, Your Highness. I wasn't... expecting you here.' Her hand shook as she clutched her handbag. When she bit her lip, Reyes smothered the memories threatening to awaken.

Turning to where his bodyguards hovered, he waved one forward. 'I have confidential business with Miss Nichols. Take her down to the basement. Until I say so, she's not allowed to contact anyone or leave the premises under any circumstances.'

'*What?* You can't do that!' She'd paled further and her breaths jerked out in shallow pants.

Reyes smiled. 'You're on Santo Sierran soil. I can do whatever I please with you.'

'But I came here to help. *Please*, Reyes—Your Highness!' she screeched as Reyes stepped back. Her fear was very real.

Reyes steeled himself against it and walked away. Never again.

He'd failed his people because of this woman.

Remembering brought a burn of pure white rage that obliterated any lingering mercy.

Even before he'd come fully awake the next morning on the yacht, he'd known something was wrong. The silence had been deafening. Complete. Where he should have heard the soft breathing and felt the warm, supple body of the lover he'd taken to his bed, there'd been a cold, empty space.

His instinct hadn't failed him. Even faced with the discovery of the theft, he'd hoped he was hallucinating. For endless minutes, he hadn't believed what he'd let happen. How much he'd let his guard down.

How spectacularly he'd failed in his duty to protect his people. That was what made the burn sting that much deeper. The full realisation that he'd taken a stranger to bed, a stranger who'd turned out to be a thief, had pointed to a singular lack of judgement, preyed on his mind like acid on metal for the last four weeks.

In the time since then Reyes could've hired a team of investigators to find and bring her to justice. But that would've served no purpose besides granting him personal satisfaction. Seeking personal vengeance, although tempting, had been relegated very low on his list. Rescuing the trade talks with Valderra had been paramount.

Of course, Mendez, handed the perfect opportunity to sink his hands deeper into the Santo Sierran coffers, had sought to do exactly that.

Relentless greed had threatened to destabilise the economy. Jasmine Nichols's actions had accelerated the process as surely as if she'd lit a fuse to a bomb.

Reyes breathed in and out, forced himself to focus through the rage and bitterness eating at him. There was no time for recriminations. For the sake of his father, for the sake of his people, he had to put personal feelings aside.

First, he would salvage the economy.

Then he would deal with Jasmine Nichols.

Jasmine pushed away the tray of tea and sandwiches. The thought of eating or even taking the smallest sip of tea made her stomach churn. She took a deep breath, folded her hands in her lap and silently prayed for strength.

The room she'd been brought to was comfortable enough. Sumptuous sofas were grouped in one corner, centred round a low antique coffee table. A conference table took up a larger space and, mounted on the far end of the wall, a large screen TV and a camera.

The red light blinked, telling her she was being observed. The memory of Reyes's cold rage slammed into her mind. Unable to sit, she jumped up. She'd been shown into this room two hours ago. Luckily, her nausea had abated but her shock and anxiety had risen in direct proportion as the realisation of what she'd walked into ate at her.

She paced, twisting her hands together. Reyes was angry and disappointed with her. No doubt about that.

She'd foolishly thought she, a junior mediator in a small-sized firm, could help rectify the situation she'd caused. Make amends for what she'd done...

Jasmine's heart lurched, a feeling of helplessness sliding over her. Reyes was probably laughing his head off at her audacity. And for all she knew, he could've already left London. The newspaper article had mentioned he was visiting several European countries to garner economic support for Santo Sierra.

If he'd truly left her to be dealt with to the fullest extent of the law, she would probably be prosecuted for treason and thrown in a Santo Sierran jail.

Her legs threatened to give way, but she forced herself to walk towards the camera. Swallowing, she looked up at the black globe.

'Can I speak to His Highness, please? I won't take up much of his time, I promise. I just... I need five minutes. Please...'

The light blinked at her.

Feeling foolish, she whirled about and paced some more. Another hour passed. Then another.

Jasmine was ready to climb the walls when the door swung open. Breath stalling, she rushed towards it. Only to stop when confronted by yet another bodyguard bearing a tray.

It held several tapas dishes, fragrant rice and a tall carafe of pomegranate juice.

'Your lunch,' the guard said in heavily accented English.

As violent as the nausea had been, the hunger cloying through her now, when the appetising smells hit her nostrils, was equally vicious. But she forced herself to shake her head. 'No. I won't eat until I speak to His Highness.'

The thickset guard blinked. Pressing home her advantage just in case she was being watched on camera, she pushed the tray away, sat on the far end of the sofa, and crossed her legs.

The door shut behind the guard. Hearing the lock turn, her insides congealed. Another half an hour passed in excruciating slowness before the handle turned again.

Reyes stood in the doorway.

The shock of seeing him again slammed into her. But she took advantage of the wider distance between them to observe him.

His face had grown haggard since Rio; perhaps it was the short designer beard he sported, his hair a little longer, shaggier. But his body was just as masculine and breathtaking as before, or even more so with the added angle of danger thrown in.

Or she could be going out of her mind, dwelling on superficial things when there was so much at stake.

'You wanted to see me.' He stepped into the room and the door shut behind him.

Now that he was here, Jasmine wasn't sure where to start. *I'm sorry* seemed so very inadequate.

So she nodded, struggling to hide the guilt eating her up inside. 'Yes. I think I can help with your...situation.'

He sucked in a sharp breath. His fingers opened and closed in a gesture of restrained control. '*Help!* You don't think you've helped enough?' he snarled.

'Please, I'm trying to make things right any way I can. Please tell me what I can do and I'll do it, Reyes—'

His eyes turned to dark pools of ice. 'You will address me as Your Highness. Addressing me by my first name was a one-time privilege. One you abused with the coarsest atrocity. And Miss Nichols?'

'Yes?'

'I suggest you eat. You won't be enjoying luxuries such as three-course meals for very much longer.'

CHAPTER FIVE

JASMINE'S BREATH SNAGGED in her throat. 'What do you mean by that?'

'I mean your situation is precarious. Once I apprise the ambassador and my council members of your crimes, your destiny will be sealed.'

'But you haven't done it yet. And you…you said earlier that the matter between us was personal.'

'I only meant I have more important matters to attend to.' His mouth compressed in a grim smile. 'You will get what's coming to you. My intention was to deal with you at a later date. I didn't think you would be foolish enough to cross my radar of your own accord just yet. So perhaps I'll watch you suffer for a long time.' His gaze went to the tray of cold food and his jaw clenched. 'You'll be brought another tray. Eat.'

He stepped towards the door.

'Wait. Please.'

'What?'

She cleared her throat. 'Will you join me for lunch? That is, if you haven't eaten yet? I can tell you why I came here while you eat? Please.'

The icy incredulity in his eyes didn't recede as he shook his head. 'You're brazen and audacious, I'll give you that. But your offer is declined, Miss Nichols,' he replied sarcastically. 'Was there anything else?'

She squeezed her eyes shut for a second. 'Please tell me what I can do to make things right. I'll do anything.'

He raised an eyebrow at her. 'I don't trust a single word out of your mouth. So I suggest you save your breath.'

She licked her lower lip and tried anyway. 'You can't leave me here for ever.'

'Can't I?' The smile that curved his lips could not in any way be described as affectionate, warm, or even cordial. The starkness of it struck pure terror in Jasmine's heart.

'I...I guess you can. But, please don't.' Her nausea was rising again. She didn't think she could stand being cooped up in here for another minute, let alone hours on end.

His shark-like smile widened, the growth of beard emphasising the feral whiteness of his teeth. A dark shiver swept over her.

'Never fear, *querida*, your sins will be addressed in due course. This subject is closed. For now.'

She'd been dismissed. Just like that. Jasmine wasn't sure which emotion—despair or trepidation—churned greater in her stomach as she watched Reyes leave. She couldn't force him to listen to the apology she'd practised for a month now. From his blatant hatred of her, she'd have to abandon any hope of asking for his forgiveness.

For now she had no recourse but to stay a prisoner.

Despair cloying through her, she paced for another hour before exhaustion deadened her limbs.

Kicking off her shoes, she sank onto the sofa. Despite the creature comforts, there were no windows in the basement. The remote for the TV had been removed. She had no idea exactly how much time had passed because her bag and phone had been taken away. The second tray Reyes had ordered delivered had also gone cold, its arrival coinciding with another case of severe nausea.

That, coupled with the exhaustion, convinced Jasmine she'd definitely picked up a bug of some sort.

Stretching out, she shivered and tried to tuck her skirt down to cover her legs as much as possible. Then, closing her eyes, she succumbed to the darkness tugging at her consciousness.

'Jasmine, wake up!'

'*Mnnnh.*' Her tongue felt too thick to convey the *no* she'd been attempting. She tried to burrow into the blanket someone had draped on her, but a sharp shake of her shoulder stopped her.

'Wake up!'

She groaned at the effort it took to pry her eyes open. 'What?'

A man, presumably a doctor from the stethoscope clinging to his neck, hovered above her. She squirmed and started to raise her hand as he shone a light in her eyes.

Sharp pain shot up her arm. 'Ouch.'

'Lie still. You have an intravenous needle in your arm.'

Reyes's deep voice was unmistakeable. Her attention swung to him as he barked at whoever else was in the room. When the volley of Spanish ceased, he was holding out a glass of water with a straw to her lips, and someone was pressing a soft pillow beneath her head.

Questions swirled in her fuzzy brain. 'Reyes…what…?'

'Don't try and speak,' he said, his eyes narrowed on her face as he addressed the doctor in Spanish.

The doctor nodded repeatedly and patted Jasmine's shoulder.

'What's he saying? What happened to me? And why do I have a needle in my arm?'

Reyes glared at her, but she saw shadows lurking in his eyes. 'You fell asleep but you didn't respond when I tried to wake you.'

The doctor spoke to Reyes. Reyes turned to her. 'Are you on any medication?'

Frowning, she shook her head. Then noticed her new surroundings for the first time. 'Where am I?'

'You're in my suite in the guest wing of the ambassador's residence.'

About to ask why she'd been relocated, she paused as the doctor addressed Reyes again. After a few minutes, the thin man bowed and left the room.

'Should I be worried that the doctor didn't want to speak to me, his patient?'

'You don't speak Spanish. And you're not a patient. You're a prisoner.'

Jasmine's temper twitched despite the knowledge that she deserved his caustic tone. She glanced at the pole next to the bed holding the IV bag. 'I know. But I'd still like to know what's wrong with me, if it's not too much trouble?' she muttered.

Reyes's mouth firmed. 'You're severely dehydrated and a touch malnourished. The fluids should do the trick. And I've ordered more food to be prepared for you. When was the last time you had a healthy meal?' he asked with a dark frown.

Her eyelids dragged heavily as she blinked. 'You mean the last time before I was incarcerated in your basement?'

'Answer the question, Jasmine.'

Her heart shouldn't have jumped at the sound of her name on his lips. But it did. 'I don't know. Yesterday afternoon, I think. I haven't had much of an appetite lately.'

Her eyes met his. Stayed. A piercing awareness lanced between them.

Reyes lunged to his feet and uttered a sharp command in Spanish. A bodyguard entered, glanced her way and nodded. She didn't need a translator to know she was the subject of the discussion. Feelings of vulnerability rose along with the hairs on her nape. 'What's going on now?'

Reyes didn't answer. He merely turned on his heel and walked through a door to a connecting room.

'His Highness requires me to attend your home...bring you a few things before we leave,' the bodyguard delivered in halting English.

Surprise froze Jasmine for all of ten seconds before her head swivelled towards the door Reyes had just walked out of. 'Leave? I'm not going anywhere.'

'You misunderstand. This is not a request from His Highness. It is a summons.'

'*A what?*' she asked dumbly, unable to immediately compute the words.

'You are required to pack a bag, *señorita*. We leave tomorrow.'

'You have your orders, I understand. But perhaps I can talk about it with *His Highness* when he has a minute?' Her words were delivered loud in the hope that Reyes would hear her from wherever he'd disappeared to. She didn't want to create any more waves, but neither could she let Reyes take over her life.

Silence descended in the room, the bodyguard eyeing her as if she'd gone insane.

Reyes re-entered the room. With a nod, he dismissed the security detail, waiting until they'd shut the door behind them before addressing her.

'I think during your exchange with my men something may have become lost in translation. My *request* was actually a command. There was nothing of a suggestion about it. When I leave here in the morning, you're coming with me.'

Despite her hammering pulse and the exhaustion sapping at her, she found the strength to speak. 'I understand that I'm your prisoner, but even prisoners get advance warning of their fate,' she implored.

One dark eyebrow rose. 'You forget you have no rights here. I hold all the cards. You go where I wish you to go.'

Jasmine's mouth dried up. The back of her hand itched and she yearned to rip the needle out, grab her shoes and handbag and run as fast as her legs could carry her. But she knew, even if her conscience allowed her, she wouldn't make it to the door.

Desperation made her blurt out, 'I have a life, a job to return to.'

'You will resign tomorrow.'

A death knell sounded somewhere in her head. 'Please, don't do this, Reyes.'

His eyes narrowed. 'Resign. Or I'll take pleasure in informing your superiors of the true depths of your character. *After* I hand you over to the authorities.'

'Are you saying that if I resign you won't tell them I'm—' She stopped, unable to speak the hated word that sealed her guilt. But he already knew she was guilty. His eyes narrowed scornfully.

'Afraid to say it out loud? *A thief*, Jasmine Nichols, that's what you are,' he condemned through clenched teeth. 'You not only stole from me, you stole from my people. You single-handedly set back years of trade negotiations.' His eyes blazed at her, grey fire that stripped her to the bone.

Her heart lurched as her sins were laid bare in front of her. The heat of shame burned through her, from the soles of her feet up through her body until the acrid taste of it flooded her mouth.

'Rey—I'm sorry. What happened wasn't supposed to happen.'

His laughter mocked her. 'You mean the sex was supposed to addle my brain so much I'd suspect someone else of the theft?' he snarled.

'No. I mean I shouldn't have taken the treaty in the first place.' Jasmine couldn't contain the sob that rose in her throat. Tears flooded her eyes. To hide it, she turned away and plugged a fist to her mouth.

But he heard it. Of course he heard it. 'Tears, Miss Nichols?' he taunted. 'How original. Almost as original as your pick-up line in Rio.'

Her sob emerged, thick and broken. Desperately, she tried to gulp it down.

His scorn reached her from across the room. 'Spare me the histrionics. You cry as if your heart is breaking. Which cannot be because you don't have a heart.'

Her head whipped round at the cruel assertion. He stood against the window, his hands shoved deep into his pockets. She deserved every accusation he threw at her, but she needed him to see she wasn't all bad.

'What I did was wrong, I know that. And I have a heart, or I wouldn't be here, trying to make amends.'

A cruel smile curved his lips. 'Well, that's a shame and a curse for you. Because I aim to make you pay for your betrayal.

And by the time I'm finished with you, you'll feel that heart you claim to possess ripped from your chest!'

Reyes watched her eyes widen. The same eyes had gazed adoringly up at him that night on his yacht, then darkened as passion had gripped them both. Eyes he'd drowned in as he'd sunk deep inside her.

Deceptive, duplicitous eyes that had taken his lust and turned it against him. Played him as a virtuoso plucked at willing strings. Deep down in a place he rarely liked to visit, it still burned him that he'd never seen it coming. That he'd been so completely and utterly duped for the second time in his life.

Duped by a woman who'd proclaimed to be one thing and turned out to be another.

And this time, the consequences threatened to be worse.

Anaïs had ruined one life, devastated one family. Jasmine's actions threatened thousands.

He'd been willing to bide his time. But he'd never been one to miss an opportunity. And while he hadn't expected the opportunity to arise so soon, he was perfectly willing to take his revenge now.

Jasmine Nichols had walked into his life, brazen and unrepentant. He had every intention of making her pay for her sins. Seeing the tears on her face only strengthened his resolve.

Reyes didn't doubt they were genuine, but he knew they were born of self-preservation rather than a show of repentance. He'd witnessed it many times before. From Anaïs. From his mother.

One hand came up and scrubbed at her face. In the blink of an eye her tears were wiped clean. As if they'd never been there. Just like in Rio. She'd charmed her way into his bed for long enough to get her hands on what she'd wanted. Then she'd vanished like a spent tornado, leaving devastation behind.

His jaw tightened. 'Who hired you to steal the treaty?' He hadn't meant to question her here, like this. But the need to know burned fiercely inside him. 'Was it Mendez?'

'No. I didn't…no one hired me.'

'So it was merely an opportunistic theft? The moment presented itself and you thought, *why not*? To what end, though? Blackmail?'

He caught her wince and felt a sliver of satisfaction. At least it showed she wasn't as unfeeling as he'd thought. Or maybe she didn't like her flaws pointed out to her. Tough. Before he was done, her every flaw would be exposed to the light of day.

She lifted a hand, as if to beseech him. 'No… Yes, it was blackmail, but you don't understand—'

He snorted. 'Theft is theft, Miss Nichols. It can't be explained away.'

The knock on the door made her jump. Reyes barked out an order and a member of staff walked in with a tray.

He took it and walked to the bed. Waiting until Jasmine sat up against the pillows, he set it down across her lap.

'I will force-feed you if necessary, but you will eat this meal, understood?' He didn't want to look at her, see how pale she was. Or remember his gut-churning anxiety when he'd been unable to wake her earlier.

Her head bowed as she looked down at the tray. 'No force-feeding necessary. I seem to have my appetite back.' Her stomach rumbled and one corner of her lush mouth lifted.

Reyes looked away and stepped back.

'Your things are being collected from your home. My plane will be ready to leave in the morning. Make sure you're packed and ready to leave.'

He headed for the door before he was tempted to do something idiotic. Like watch her eat.

CHAPTER SIX

'IS THERE REALLY no other way for me to make amends?'

Reyes took the empty tray and handed it to the member of staff hovering nearby.

'No.'

He glimpsed a touch of rebellion in her eyes and something fizzed through his blood, almost an anticipation of his battle with her. Which was curious. And ridiculous. All he was interested in was making her pay for her actions. 'You'll come with me—'

'Or you'll report me to the authorities? Have me thrown in jail?' Her fingers twisted in her lap. 'I know. Maybe that's a better option than...'

'Facing my brand of justice? You know, I think that's the first sensible decision you've made since we met. But seriously, do you want to take your chances locked in the basement again? You didn't last half a day. The bureaucracy before you're brought to trial alone would take months, if not years. On the other hand, a Santo Sierran prison is so much better. We deliver justice swiftly. If nothing else, you'll have wall-to-wall sunshine all year round; you can acquire a permanent tan during your lifelong incarceration.'

Fear clenched her heart. 'Is that where we—you're going?'

'Eventually. You have until morning to decide. Then I abandon you to the ambassador's mercy.'

She paled further. 'I've suffered worse, I'm sure. But I really don't think it needs to come to that.'

Surprise sparked through Reyes at her reply, then he berated himself for his reaction. Obviously his wasn't the first threat of punishment Jasmine Nichols had received in her life. Curious, he regarded her. How many other men had she tricked with her body, then stolen from? How many others had fallen for her sensual beauty? Been duped by the promise of her *bed-me* eyes and silken skin?

Anger rose inside him.

The need to deliver his own brand of justice grew stronger. Needing to turn up the heat, he stalked closer. 'You mentioned your family,' he started conversationally. 'Do they know you're a thief?'

Her colour receded a little more, her full lips firming just a tiny fraction. Satisfaction coursed through him.

'Will they be prepared to lose everything they have in order to make reparations to the Santo Sierran people?'

She drew in a sharp breath. 'This has *nothing* to do with my family.'

'That's where you're wrong, Jasmine. You wronged *my people*, my *family*. It is only right that you *and* your family make the appropriate amends.'

'No! Please—'

'A simple phone call is all it would take to round them all up. Santo Sierra has extradition treaties with the United Kingdom—'

'No. I meant what I said. It doesn't have to come to that.'

'So you would prefer me to leave your family out of this?'

Her lips worked for several tense seconds, which stretched to a full minute. Then a sigh of defeat escaped her parted lips. 'Is it worth me saying anything else but that I would like you to leave my family alone?'

He took a deep breath. And smiled. 'No.'

'Then I'll…come with you…wherever you want me to.'

He turned and walked out of the room. Jasmine set her cutlery down and tried to think through the roller-coaster speed of her thoughts. In the end, she could only hope she'd made the right decision.

Sunset bathed the hills in orange and red as their car climbed the roads leading to Reyes's Spanish hacienda. Jasmine had long given up any hope of trying to memorise her whereabouts. All she knew was that they were somewhere deep in Northern Spain.

They'd long left behind the tourist traps and sandy beaches of Barcelona. Here the houses were few and far between, with occasional villages flashing past before she could take meaningful note of where she was.

Reyes sat beside her but he might as well have been thousands of miles away. A pair of designer sunglasses shielded his eyes from her and the phone he'd commandeered since boarding his plane remained glued to one ear.

From the snatches of conversation she'd heard, he was planning several more meetings with government ministers and his own council here in Spain.

Looking carefully, she could see the signs of strain around his mouth and the skin pulled taut over his cheekbones, but he was very much a man in command.

Sensing her scrutiny, he swivelled his head in her direction. A second later, he ended his call.

'Where exactly are we going?' she enquired.

'To my estate in Zaragoza,' he replied in a clipped tone.

'And…how long will we be staying there?'

'As long as it takes. If you have any aspirations of escape, kill them now.'

She clasped her hand in her lap, refusing to rise to his baiting. 'My family will be worried if I don't let them know how long I'll be away,' she tried to reason with him.

Her mother had been confused when she'd called to say she was taking a holiday and had no idea when she would be returning. Stephen had been even more difficult to convince. Jasmine had been avoiding him since her return from Rio, but she knew her stepfather suspected she'd had something to do with him being suddenly free of debt and the prospect of jail.

'And you always strive to maintain the appearance of a dutiful daughter, do you?' Scorn poured from Reyes, the naked censure in his voice stinging her skin. 'Obviously, you've succeeded in pulling the wool over their eyes all these years.'

Jasmine bit back her retort to the contrary. It *was* because of her past that her mother worried when she didn't hear from her daughter. The past she'd tried so hard to escape from but had stepped firmly back into with her one wrong decision in Rio.

Finding no adequate words to defend herself, she kept silent. With an impatient movement, Reyes ripped the glasses from his eyes and caught her chin in his hand. Jasmine found herself locked into his intense gaze.

'Are you going to speak or do you intend to play mute?' he asked.

'I don't really have anything to say to you.'

He folded the glasses and slipped them into his shirt pocket. 'Your father, Stephen Nichols, works for the British government, does he not?'

His announcement startled her. His eyes held rigid ice that threatened to stop the blood flow in her veins. 'He's my stepfather, but how…what does that have to do with anything?' Her instinct warned she wouldn't like the path this conversation was taking.

'I'm merely trying to form a picture in my head. And your mother…what does she do?'

Jasmine licked dry lips, her thoughts churning as she debated the wisdom of evading his questions. In the end, she decided withholding the information would serve no useful purpose. 'She's his PA.'

'So to all intents and purposes, they're both upstanding citizens?' he asked, one dark eyebrow raised.

Her pulse increased as her gaze followed the graceful arch of his brow. Even when her eyes dropped to encounter his frozen regard, her pulse still thundered. Because deep inside, Jasmine knew his questions weren't as innocuous as he'd couched them.

She tried not to let him see how much he riled her. 'If you have a point, please state it.'

'I'm just wondering how come you've strayed so far from the righteous path.'

She flinched. 'I beg your pardon?'

His teeth bared in a semblance of a smile, but all it did was send a wave of dread over her. 'I'm trying to understand you, *querida*. How a woman such as you, with a seemingly stable background and upbringing, ends up being a thief.'

'You know nothing about me, except for an impression you think you got from us spending a few hours together. I can understand how what I did would colour your judgement, but that's far from the whole picture.'

His face hardened. 'I *know* you were instrumental in demolishing my country's trade treaty. You don't think that's enough?' he finished on a snarl.

Remembering how she'd felt when she saw the headline announcing the breakdown of talks, Jasmine slid her gaze from his. 'I'm sorry. But technically, Mendez is also responsible—'

'And since all evidence points to you working for Mendez, isn't the conclusion the same?' he sneered.

Her head snapped round to his. '*No!* You're wrong. I don't work for Mendez. I've never even met the man!'

'Really? You work as a broker and a mediator, do you not?'

Puzzled, she nodded.

'And over the past three years, your specialty has been in brokering agreements in Latin American companies?'

Her frown deepened in direct proportion to the escalation of her dread. 'How do you know all this?'

He continued as if she hadn't spoken. 'When we met you told me you'd been watching the Santo-Valderran talks *with interest*.'

Jasmine found his reasoning difficult to comprehend. 'And you think by interest I meant to sabotage it? For what purpose?'

'What other purpose could there be aside from financial?'

'Feel free to search my finances. You'd be surprised to find I'm not as flush as you think I am.'

'You're too intelligent to display the fruits of your duplicity. Are you so confident that I won't find the evidence I need if I cast my net a little wider, like, say, your parents?'

Jasmine felt the blood drain from her face. Despite her bravado, the last thing she wanted was for Reyes to start digging into Stephen's affairs. The evidence of his gambling, misappropriation and connection to people like Joaquin Esteban would become public knowledge if Reyes took that route.

Her stepfather had been visibly shaken by his ordeal at the hands of Joaquin's men, enough to induce an angina attack that had laid him up in hospital for a week.

Unfortunately, it had taken that experience to wake him up to his dangerous addiction. He had just started a programme to help overcome his gambling problem; the last thing she wanted was for his life to be thrown into turmoil by Reyes.

Watching him struggle to overcome his weakness, she'd been reminded of what Stephen himself had said to her years earlier.

Nobody was perfect.

She'd reminded herself of that over and over again in the last four weeks. Except she was sure, when it came to Prince Reyes Navarre, that belief wouldn't hold water.

She tried to remain calm as Reyes, sensing her turmoil, tilted her face up to his.

'I see I've stumbled onto something. Who were the beneficiaries if not your parents?' His fingers tightened. 'Your lover?'

With excruciating effort, she wrenched herself free. 'What does it matter? I did it,' she admitted, not seeing the point in prolonging the agony.

Beside her, he tensed. Her fingers clenched in her lap, the rush of memories threatening to eat her alive. Desperately, she tried to push them away, but they pushed back. Hard.

I did it. This wasn't the first time she'd said those words. But she'd hoped back then it would be the last. How wrong she'd been.

Squeezing her eyes shut for a single heartbeat, she took a deep breath, opened them and tried to plead with Reyes.

'I did it. I'm willing to take the consequences. Just tell me what I need to do.' Because the earlier she could make reparations, the earlier she could put him behind her.

CHAPTER SEVEN

REYES FOUND HIMSELF riveted by the frank admission, unable to look away from the open candour in Jasmine's face as she looked back at him. For the first time in his life, he found himself speechless.

I did it.

In all the imagined scenarios when he'd dreamed of exacting his revenge, not once had he entertained the notion that she would admit her guilt so readily.

He wondered why he was surprised. Weren't her audacity, her sheer bolshiness what had attracted him a month ago in Rio? Yet even now, Reyes could see that her reaction, while mostly convincing, was just a front. But a front that hid what? What was Jasmine Nichols keeping from him?

He continued to stare at her. She stared back, her gaze unflinching. Against his will, he felt his blood firing up, his heartbeat quicken. Shifting in his seat, he sat back, took a deep breath.

Jasmine had made things easy for him. He now didn't need to bother with interrogating her. She'd admitted her guilt and he had her confession. Her punishment would wait until he'd dealt with more important matters.

'*Gracias,*' he murmured, breaking eye contact. The strange sense of loss he felt was immediately pushed aside.

'What are you thanking me for?' she asked.

'Saving me the time and energy of interrogating you. Who did you give the treaty to?'

She shook her head. 'I can't tell you that.'

'You're wrong. When the time is right you'll give me a name. Every person responsible for this chaos will be brought to justice.'

Despite the fire in her eyes, she swallowed and looked away.

His car swung into the last stretch of road leading to his estate and a sense of satisfaction stole over him. In London, he'd felt at a slight loss; that control wasn't totally within his grasp. Within touching distance of the place he called his second home, his control returned.

San Estrela was his mother's birthplace and where she had married his father. Reyes had maybe one or two fairly happy holidays here as a child…until everything had turned sour. He wouldn't be creating any more happy memories by bringing his prisoner here, but he had no choice.

As much as it burned him to admit it, he couldn't yet return to Santo Sierra. He needed to rally economic support in order to get the talks with Valderra back on track. Plus, at present, he wasn't entirely sure whom he could trust in his own council.

His insides clenched as he thought of his father. Ruthlessly, he pushed the feeling aside. If he was to achieve what he was aiming for, he needed to clear his mind of his grief; of making things right with the father he'd lost for so long. Ironically, it was his own downfall with Jasmine Nichols that had made Reyes see his father in a different light. To not judge the old man so harshly for his own mistakes.

He would return to his father's bedside soon enough. Make amends. Hopefully before it was too late.

He alighted from the car and automatically held out his hand. Jasmine took it and straightened beside him a second later. He dropped her hand, not wanting to acknowledge how her skin felt against his.

A frown crossed her face before she masked it.

Reyes didn't know what to do with that look. On the one hand, she remained stoic in the face of her guilt, yet on the other she looked at him with contrition. The enigma unsettled and irritated him.

Pushing aside the feeling, he mounted the stairs as the door swung open to reveal his major-domo, Armando. The man wore the same anxious look he'd seen on so many Santo Sierran faces.

Reminded that his people were living in a state of constant worry made Reyes's chest tighten.

Knowing the cause of all this turmoil stood two steps behind him made his blood simmer as he greeted Armando.

'This is Miss Jasmine Nichols. She'll be my guest for the duration of my stay. She is, however, not permitted to leave the house or grounds under any circumstances. If she attempts to leave, use all means necessary to prevent her,' he instructed.

'You don't need to do that. I know why I'm here. You have my word that I won't run away.'

'You'll forgive me if I don't find your *word* reassuring?'

She inhaled sharply. 'I suppose I deserve that,' she murmured.

Reyes frowned at the hurt in her voice.

Armando, his usual capable, unruffled self, barely blinked at the exchange. 'I will put her in the Valencia Suite, Your Highness.'

'No, the Leon Suite next to mine will suffice.'

'Very well, Your Highness.'

Reyes turned down the hall towards his study and had barely taken half a dozen steps when he heard the click of heels racing after him.

He stopped. 'Did you want something?'

She looked pale, her face creased in concern as her eyes fell. When she began to visibly tremble, Reyes frowned. She hadn't been well yesterday, but she'd reassured the doctor this morning that she was fine.

'What do you mean by any means necessary?' she asked.

'Stay in the house and within the grounds and you'll never have to find out. Understood?'

A tinge of relief brought colour to her cheeks. Reyes didn't realise how disconcerting her paleness was until she regained her composure.

She shook her head. 'I can't just do nothing. I'll go out of my mind.'

'That's your punishment for now. Do otherwise and I'll have to revise my decision.'

She sighed. 'Rey—I mean, Your Highness.' Her hand lifted, as if to touch him. 'Can I have my phone back? Please, I need to let my parents know where I am. My mother will send the cavalry out in full force if I don't, and, trust me, you don't want that.' A small, wistful smile touched her lips.

The idea of her delusional mother, sitting snug in her home, worrying about her perfect daughter, made his teeth clench. No doubt Jasmine had succeeded in pulling the wool over her parents' eyes the way she'd done with him. And yet the thought of the perfect family picture all that *togetherness* presented sent a dart of something very close to jealousy through him.

He'd never had a parent worry over him like that. His mother had been too caught up in trying to turn his father's existence into a living hell to worry about the two children who'd needed her attention. And his father had been too busy turning himself inside out for a faithless woman. Reyes had been a young boy when he'd realised there wouldn't be any scrap of attention from either of his parents.

It was the reason boarding school had been a relief. It was the reason he'd chosen not to form attachments to any woman. Sex for the sake of it had been his mantra.

Until Anaïs. Until his mother's death.

After that even sex hadn't mattered.

Nothing had mattered. Nothing but duty.

Feeling the bitterness encroach, Reyes whirled and stalked towards his study. 'See Armando. He'll show you where the phone is. But one call is all you get. Make it count.'

Jasmine ended the call to her mother and put the phone down in the seriously gorgeous solarium Armando had shown her into. She took a calming breath and looked around her. Outside, a carpet of rich green grass rolled away towards a stand of cypress trees at the bottom of the valley they'd climbed out of. To the right, a more cultivated garden, hedged with roses, bougainvillea and hyacinths grew beyond a sun-washed terrace. She stood for a moment, letting the sun and stunning surroundings wash over her.

As prisons went, this one wasn't so bad, she mused. Although if she had to compare jailors, she would've preferred one who didn't make her pulse jump, who didn't make her wish her path to this place had been different.

In the car earlier, she'd refused to give Joaquin's name, partly because of what it would mean for her stepfather. But she'd also shied away from the conversation because she'd been afraid Reyes would find out about her past. That he'd discover that the woman he'd taken to bed had grown up in a council estate and been nearly initiated into a drug-dealing gang. That she had a juvenile record she'd never be able to erase.

He might detest her now, but that was far better than his repulsion, his scorn.

The chirp of a bird steered her from another unwanted trip down memory lane. She'd been taking those trips far too often these last weeks. Ever since that night in Rio, in fact. She needed to snap out of it. Put it behind her.

She would face whatever punishment Reyes chose to dole out on her, but the past belonged in the past.

A sound from behind her made her turn.

Armando entered, pushing a trolley laden with food. 'I do not know the *señorita's* preference, so I have brought a selection.'

She'd missed breakfast again because she hadn't been able to stomach any of the food the embassy had laid out for them this morning. Lately, any thought of food made her stomach roil. So she approached the trolley cautiously. And breathed easier once she could look at the mouthwatering selection of *tapas* without turning green.

Perhaps telling the doctor she was fine this morning had been a mistake...

Thanking Armando, she heaped her plate with bread, ham, and a green salad and took a seat at the dining area near the window. She polished off the food in record time and went back for seconds, adding plump olives marinated in chilli oil.

She was about to pick up her cutlery when Reyes strolled in. Without a word, he selected his own food, then pulled up a chair opposite her.

In low tones, he dismissed Armando and shook out his napkin.

'So,' he started conversationally, 'you told your mother I was your boyfriend.' It wasn't a question. It was an observation, marred with thick layers of distaste.

Jasmine's appetite fled. Her cutlery dropped noisily onto the table. 'How did you know that?'

One sleek brow arched. 'Did I not mention it? All incoming and outgoing calls from San Estrela are monitored. And yes, I have a zero-trust policy where you're concerned.'

Despite the heat engulfing her face at the pointed remark, she met his gaze head-on. 'If you were listening then you would've heard that my mother *assumed* you were my boyfriend. I didn't—'

'Correct that assumption. You've been caught in yet another lie, Miss Nichols. It's quite astonishing how they trip so easily from your lips.' His gaze dropped to her lips and she felt a guilty tingle as if he'd branded her mouth with just that one look.

'I could hardly tell her I was being held prisoner somewhere in Northern Spain!'

He ripped a piece of bread in half, dipped it in his olive oil and took a healthy bite. 'Maybe you should have. For her own good, she needs to know she doesn't have the perfect daughter she seems to think she does.'

'You don't know me and you don't know my mother, so don't presume to judge us. Besides, what makes you think she believes I'm perfect?'

'She must do. She seemed to eat up all the lies you fed her without question.'

Jasmine was tempted to tell Reyes of her mother's one fatal flaw—she refused to see the bad in anyone. Her blindly trusting nature had seen her duped out of her money over and over by ruthless men. It was that nature that had landed them where Jasmine had been forced down a path of near permanent ruin.

It was a place Jasmine didn't like to remind her mother of, or ever revisit herself, if she could help it.

'It's easier for my mother to take things at face value.' Her words emerged with much more bitter introspection than she'd intended. Aware of just how much she'd let slip, Jasmine clamped her jaw shut and tried not to even breathe. But it was too late.

Reyes's head cocked to the side in the now oh-so-familiar way. 'Interesting. She knows and she accepts you just the way you are?' The way he said it, almost wistfully, drew her gaze to him.

He was staring at her and yet she got the feeling his mind was somewhere else altogether. Somewhere he didn't want to relive, but couldn't seem to help.

She picked up her fork and speared an olive. A quick whiff of it had her setting it down again. She tried a piece of ham and chewed that instead. After swallowing, she answered, 'Yes, she does. She likes to think that people change. So do I, incidentally.'

As if snapping out of whatever place he'd been, he sharpened his gaze. 'No, they don't. They like to pretend they do. Some do their best to present a different face to the world, but people inherently remain the same underneath.'

'I don't believe that.'

'Why, because *you've* changed? You've somehow seen some mystic light and repented all your sins?'

She swallowed. 'Yes.'

'We both know that's not true, don't we, Jasmine? Otherwise you wouldn't have stolen from me.'

'I had no choice.'

His jaw tightened. 'You had a choice. You made the wrong one.'

After a moment, she nodded. 'Yes, maybe you're right.'

Her answer silenced him for several moments, his speculative gaze on her face. 'And how many times have you made the wrong choice in the past?'

'My past is none of your business.' And not a place she chose to willingly visit. The stigma of being judged was one she'd learned from when her college boyfriend had treated her like a pariah when she'd confessed her past. 'I'm more concerned about the future. If you're going to hand me over to the authorities, I'd prefer it to be sooner rather than later.'

His face slowly hardened into the mask she detested, but had unfortunately become very familiar with. 'Don't push me, Jasmine. If you didn't steal from me for yourself, tell me who you did it for.'

Her heart lurched. 'I can't. Punish me, if you need to, but leave anyone else out of it.'

'Why?'

'Because the person I did it for is important to me.'

'How important?' he flung back.

'He…saved me. He didn't have to, but he did. I'm sorry, Re—Your Highness, but I won't let him pay for my mistakes.'

'So this person saved you, but decided it was okay to set you back on a destructive path to suit his purposes?'

'No, it wasn't like that.'

His hand slammed down. 'That was exactly what it was, Jasmine. To trap me so you could steal from me. From my people. To throw years of hard work into utter chaos and endanger the livelihood of millions, all for the sake of one person.'

'Yes, I know it seems irrational but that's what happened. Believe me, I'll do anything to make things right.'

He relaxed in his seat with the grace of a born predator, his long, rangy frame seeming to go on for ever. His smile held no mirth, only cynicism. 'How bravely you embrace your sins. It's almost admirable.'

She set her fork down. 'Stop toying with me and just get this over and done with.'

His smile widened, his teeth stark against the darkness of his beard. For some reason, the sight made her belly flip over. Whether it was from fear or another emotion, Jasmine didn't want to examine too closely.

'You're not in a position to dictate terms to me, Miss Nichols. Remember, you're *my* prisoner. *I* will choose the time of your trial. And the terms of your punishment. Push me and you'll like the consequences of either even less.'

Over the next four days she barely saw Reyes. She caught glimpses of him—as he paced the terrace just before the midday sun hit full blast, or as Armando took a tray into his study. Once she looked down from her window early in the morning and saw him swimming, his powerful strokes carrying him from one end of the enormous pool to the other.

Voyeuristically, she watched him, unable to look away from his magnificent, streamlined body. When he heaved himself out of the pool and scrubbed a towel through his wet hair, desire settled low and heavy in her belly.

As she lay in bed now, remembering how that body had felt up close against hers in Rio drenched her whole body in sensation. Ashamed, she flipped over, punched her frustration into a pillow and pulled the covers over herself as if her actions would block out the feelings.

But being in bed only reminded her of another bed, where their bodies had writhed, strained into each other as they'd ridden the storm of passion breaking over them.

Unnerved by the sheer depth of her riotous feelings, Jasmine threw back the covers and jumped out of bed.

Too late, she remembered that, lately, her mornings were best approached gingerly. Rushing to the bathroom, she vomited until her eyes stung.

Afterwards, clutching the sink, her fingers dug into the cold porcelain as she calculated dates and tried not to panic. She'd had her period two weeks ago, albeit a lighter than usual one.

And Reyes had used condoms in Rio. Hadn't he?

No, it was all in her head. Being cooped up in San Estrela was making her stir-crazy!

Today she was going to offer Reyes whatever input she thought would help with salvaging the treaty. Failing that, she'd ask him what he intended to do with her. This suspended limbo was sending her imagination into overdrive.

Why else would she think she could be pregnant with Reyes's baby? The very thought made her tremble.

Quickly showering, she dressed in a light blue sleeveless linen dress with a tan belt and slipped her feet into tan heels. Brushing her hair and tying it loosely at her nape, she massaged a small amount of sun protection into her skin and face and left her suite.

Carmelita, the housekeeper, was carrying a large bale of towels towards the guest suites in the west wing when Jasmine reached the top of the stairs. About to ask the whereabouts of Reyes, Jasmine paused at the sound of male voices in the hallway.

Reyes strolled into view, accompanied by four men. The first thing she noticed was that his beard was gone. A tiny, completely unprepared and shocking part of her mourned that she'd never got to experience the rasp of his facial hair against her skin.

The second thing she noticed was that all the men wore suits. And that she was the sole focus of their attention as she stood, poised, at the top of the stairs.

A block of silence passed.

Reyes turned to the men, his voice low. Without glancing her way, he led them to his study and shut the door with a firm click.

Jasmine stood rooted to the step, unable to move. She wasn't sure why she was so hurt that she'd been dismissed like a piece of trash.

What did she expect?

She was a prisoner here. Barely worth the food or accommodation she took up. Did she really expect Reyes to introduce her as his guest?

With leaden feet, she came down the stairs and went onto the terrace, where she usually breakfasted.

Carmelita brought her fresh coffee. She helped herself to a slice of toast and a plump orange, but her mind churned. When Carmelita emerged again to clear away the dishes, Jasmine's curiosity got the better of her.

'Who are those men with His Highness?' she asked casually.

The housekeeper looked uncomfortable for a moment, then she replied, 'One is the Santo Sierra *embajador* to France. Other men are from Santo Sierra.'

'How long have they been here?'

'They came late last night.' She bustled about, hurriedly gathering the used tableware.

Unwilling to question her any further, Jasmine left her in peace. Clearly, her meeting with Reyes would have to take a backseat to his meeting with his ambassador and council. But she needed something, *anything* to stop her thinking of what her past week's morning sickness meant.

Because if her suspicions were true…then…*oh, God!*

Going back to fetch her sunglasses, Jasmine came downstairs and let herself out through the solarium.

She bypassed the gardens and headed for the trees. In a distant past, she'd harboured a secret wish to be a gardener. That was before another one of her mother's liaisons had run off with her savings and they'd ended up in a tower block, where the only green in sight had been from the bile-coloured paint on the walls.

Jasmine had been only six at the time, but she'd vowed never to let her emotions blind her the way her mother did. In fact she'd killed off all her emotions…until Stephen had forced her to face them. To choose a better life than the one she'd been contemplating at seventeen.

She trailed her fingers over the expertly pruned foliage and imagined herself tending the plants and trees all year round.

Spotting a greenhouse at the end of a row of hedges, Jasmine veered towards it.

Before she could turn the handle, heavy footsteps pounded the ground behind her. In a heartbeat, Armando and two of Reyes's bodyguards had surrounded her. One bodyguard took her by the arm and marched her towards the villa.

'What are you doing? Let go of me!'

He didn't respond. Back indoors, she managed to rip herself from the guard's grasp as the door to the study flew open.

Jasmine stared at a fuming Reyes, refusing to cower under his oppressive stare.

'I thought we had an agreement.' His grey eyes flashed with barely suppressed anger.

She massaged her stinging elbow. 'The agreement still holds. I haven't run away, have I?'

'You left the house without permission.'

'To go to the garden! I'm going insane cooped up in your gilded prison. How did you know I'd left the house anyway?'

'Every time a door is opened in the house, an alarm goes off in the security suite. My men alerted me.' His gaze dropped to where she was nursing her elbow. His face grew darker. 'Why are you rubbing your elbow? Are you hurt?'

'Do you care?'

He glared at her for several seconds. Then, turning to his bodyguard, he murmured a few words.

Jasmine's heart twisted, then thundered in outrage when she saw what was being handed to Reyes.

'No! If you dare come near me with that thing, I'll—'

'You'll what? Scream? Go ahead. Give it your best shot.' He stepped closer, the handcuffs gleaming in his hands.

Memories, the worst kind of memories, crowded her mind,

pushing fear up through her belly into her chest. Her breath shortened. 'No, Reyes— No, don't. Please!'

Hyperventilating, she tried to step back. Her feet wouldn't move. The blood drained out of her head as she fought to breathe. Her head grew woozy with fog. She started to sway.

'If you insist on disobeying me, this is your only—Jasmine?'

His voice wove in and out. She blinked, fighting the light-headedness. Damn, either she really was unwell, or she was turning into a pathetic shadow of herself around this man.

Either way, it had to stop!

CHAPTER EIGHT

'JASMINE!'

Reyes caught her by the arms and watched her pull herself together. She'd gone deathly pale at the sight of the handcuffs and for a moment he'd thought she would pass out.

She continued to stare at the restraints as if they were poisonous serpents ready to strike at her.

She willingly admitted to being a criminal yet the sight of handcuffs terrified her. Surely she was used to them by now?

Puzzled, he slipped the cuffs into his back pocket and dismissed his bodyguard. Her trembling had increased and even though she tried to hide it, he caught the haunted look in her eyes.

Dios, something had happened to her.

'Jasmine.'

She didn't move. Didn't react. It was almost as if she hadn't heard him. Stepping closer, he gripped her tighter. Felt her tremble. An unwelcome emotion shifted through his chest.

'You will respond when I address you.'

Her reaction was immediate. She wrenched herself from him, almost violently. Eyes wide, she glared at him, but he was sure her consciousness was elsewhere.

'No! I won't let you use those things on me!'

'It's fine. It's okay,' he murmured, brushing her soft, silky cheek. He realised what he was doing and removed his hand, puzzled and annoyed with himself for offering comfort where he should be doling out punishment.

She stared at the hand suspended between them. Then she searched for the handcuffs before her wide, frightened eyes darted back to his face.

'Do you want to tell me what just happened?' he asked.

She sucked in a shaky breath and gathered herself with that strength of will he couldn't help but admire. 'I have no idea what you're talking about.'

A cold hand clamped around Reyes's neck. How many times had he heard his mother utter those same words? When he'd demanded to know what she was doing in the papers being photographed in the arms of a man other than his father...when Reyes had confronted her about the alcohol on her breath or the hazy look in her eyes, she'd always uttered those words.

I have no idea what you're talking about, Reyes. Don't be so fanciful, Reyes.

'So you deny that the sight of the restraints disturbed you? Then you won't mind if I use—'

She tried to snatch her hands away. 'No. Don't use it. I promise...I won't leave the villa.'

He was dying to know what had happened to her. But not so badly that he wanted to be lied to. He might have tried to fool himself into believing that it didn't matter, but Jasmine's untruths somehow managed to get under his skin. Sting that little harder.

'Your promises are worthless to me—surely you know that by now? So I'm afraid you'll have to do more than that.'

She swallowed. 'What do you mean?'

Reyes stepped back and indicated the door to his study. 'You'll stay where I can keep an eye on you.'

'So I guess a request for a trip into town is out of the question?'

Reyes let his cool stare speak for him.

She rolled her eyes before her gaze dropped to his pockets, where the cuffs were hidden out of sight. 'Fine. I'll go and find a book to read.'

For some reason, Reyes couldn't suppress a smile as she firmed her lips and sent him a glance of pure loathing.

He stopped her as she stepped past him. 'Wait.'

Surprised, she looked up. Then frowned. 'What now?'

Reyes grasped her elbow and examined where she'd rubbed

it before. Faint marks marred her skin. A touch of fury flared within him. He would be having words with his bodyguard later. 'You didn't tell me whether you were hurt or not?' he repeated his earlier question. *Why was that so important to him?* He stemmed the mocking voice and waited for her answer.

'It's nothing I haven't endured before.' As if realising her slip, she bit her lip.

The memory of doing the same to those lips, and much more, slammed into him. His groin stirred to life. Smashing it down, he concentrated on her words.

'You've been manhandled before?' The very thought made something tug hard in his chest.

'Not without fighting back, I can assure you.' The blaze of defiance and determination flared higher in her eyes.

He wasn't reassured. Intrigued, he stared at her for a long time before he could form the words. 'You will not be treated like that under my roof. Be assured of that.'

'So what do you call using those handcuffs tucked away in your pocket? An early Christmas present?'

His mouth twisted. 'Perhaps I should rephrase that. No one but I will be allowed to touch you while you're under my roof.'

'Well, that makes me feel heaps better.' Despite the bravado in her voice, a dart of apprehension crossed her eyes.

About to reassure her again that she would come to no harm, he stopped himself. Reminded himself of what this woman had done. To him. To his country.

Right at this moment, he had members of Santo Sierra's council in his study, trying to find a way out of their current predicament. So far they seemed to be agreed on only one course of action. One that Reyes was determined not to give in to.

Meanwhile, here he was trying to placate the woman responsible for causing the turbulence in his kingdom.

Twisting on his heel, he barked, 'Come.'

'You want me at your meeting?'

'I want you where I can keep an eye on you.'

He heard her footsteps behind him as he entered his study. Two of his advisors gaped at his guest. The third, most senior of them, frowned as Reyes shut the door and directed Jasmine into the seat in the corner of the room.

His senior advisor shifted in his seat. 'Your Highness, what we're discussing is highly confidential. I hardly think it appropriate to have a stranger—'

'Miss Nichols is here as my guest. She won't divulge anything we say in this room.' He looked at her. She read the clear warning and nodded.

He sat down but not before his gaze caught her bare legs as she crossed them. Again heat lanced his groin. Those legs had curled around his waist, urged him on as he'd thrust inside her.

Inside her duplicitous body...

He cleared his throat and shifted in his seat. 'You said you know how many people were thinking of backing the new treaty?' he addressed his senior advisor.

Costanzo Alvarez nodded. 'It is currently seven to nine, Your Highness. With each day that passes, the older members are being swayed to the idea of the original treaty your father agreed to sign.'

Reyes's hackles rose. 'Those terms are no longer on the table. The new treaty will create at least another five thousand jobs.'

Alvarez shook his head. 'Mendez won't sign the new treaty, and Santo Sierra needs economic stability sooner rather than later. Any delay in providing that stability is a delay we can't afford.'

His second advisor leaned forward. 'As Costanzo said, stability is what will steer the people into calmer waters. I think Santo Sierrans are more afraid than anything else of what the future holds—'

'Make your point,' Reyes cut across him.

'Should you marry and produce an heir quickly, it'll restore the people's faith in—'

'Are you seriously suggesting that the only way to please

the people is to marry? I'm supposed to be garnering economic support for Santo Sierra, not hunting Europe for a bride.'

'Santo Sierra has always thrived in direct proportion to how well its monarchy is thriving. With your father's health in rapid decline, the people are worried about their future, yes, but they're also worried about you.'

Reyes frowned. 'So I'm to conjure up a bride out of thin air, marry her and produce an heir instead of pursuing our economic growth?'

Alvarez tented his fingers. 'No reason why you can't do both. But we suggest you do it more…visibly. You've always been a private person, Your Highness. Even when you're in Santo Sierra you're hardly seen. Besides the council, most people believe you've been at the King's bedside for the past few weeks. Only a handful of people know differently.'

Reyes shook his head. 'Even if I agree to this plan, even if I calm my people for a while, we still need to bring Mendez to the table to sign another treaty.'

He heard a muffled sound and glanced at Jasmine. Her eyes met his and he read the bleak apology in them.

He wanted to believe her. Wanted to believe she was anywhere near sorry for the wrongs she'd done. But he'd let himself be fooled in the past. Let his guard down enough to believe his mother's lies.

Each time, she'd stabbed him with savage lies and callous indifference. She'd done the same to his father. Reyes and his sister had watched their father, the King of Santo Sierra, wither with each deception, each act of adultery.

And yet, if Jasmine was to believed, she'd done it not for personal gain, but to save someone she cared about. She'd sacrificed her safety, her reputation for the sake of another…

The curious tug at his chest made him tense. There was no redemption in what Jasmine had done. He was a fool to look for any.

* * *

Jasmine bit her lip as Reyes turned away. His whole body bristled in rejection of her silent apology.

She looked down at the file she'd picked up as the men talked. She refused to acknowledge that dart of discomfort that had lodged itself in her heart when the idea of Reyes marrying had been brought up.

It had nothing to do with her. She had no claim on him. She never would. She was only in this room because Reyes didn't trust her to wander his house without making a run for it.

Once he'd decided what her punishment was to be, she would serve it and be done. The fate of his country was his to deal with as he saw fit.

And yet…

Reyes…married to a princess befitting his station. An equal who would complement his heritage, who would have his babies and be gifted the privilege of waking up next to him for the rest of her life.

Her throat tightened. This time the bile that rose had nothing to do with nausea and everything to do with blind, raging jealousy.

Gripping the file, she forced herself to read the copy of the trade treaty that she'd handed to Joaquin.

Each kingdom had agreed to supply resources to one another. On execution, the two kingdoms would have combined power equivalent to the United Arab Emirates' control of the world's oil and steel. Despite Santo Sierra being the smaller kingdom, it held the richer resource. No wonder Mendez had his greedy eyes set on it.

Jasmine finished reading and closed the file.

This was what she'd wrecked.

The trade agreement would have created thousands of jobs, made countless lives better. She'd jeopardised all those lives to save one.

Caught between the fresh vice of guilt and the loyalty that

wouldn't be snuffed out, she wrapped her arms around herself. Then, unable to sit still, she jumped up.

'Let me help. Please…'

Four sets of eyes slashed to her. Condemnation. Bitterness. Curiosity. Contemptuous dismissal. All expressions she'd seen before displayed through varied gazes when she was growing up.

Seeing most of those in Reyes's eyes, she felt a lance of hurt pierce her heart.

What had she expected? That he would simply forget that she was the reason he was here, now, instead of back in his kingdom?

She cleared her throat as their gazes continued to sear her. 'I've assisted in a few international brokerage deals that—'

'Excuse me, Miss…?' Costanzo Alvarez glared at her.

She bit back a retort and breathed deep. 'Jasmine Nichols,' she replied.

He gave a curt nod. He looked at the youngest advisor at the table. The man gave a subtle nod and started tapping the tablet keyboard in front of him.

'What we're dealing with here isn't a petty squabble between two fashion houses. Or a divorce settlement where you decide who gets to keep the prized goldfish. We're dealing with—'

'I know what you're dealing with,' she retorted.

'Then perhaps you should sit down and—'

'Let her speak.' A low, terse command from Reyes.

Jasmine looked at him. His eyes were narrowed, displeasure weaving through the grey depths. But he wasn't displeased enough to instruct her to be quiet, which was a small blessing. Or perhaps he was waiting for her to make a fool of herself so he could mock her some more?

She licked her lips.

His gaze followed the movement. Electricity zapped her spine as she recalled how the potency of his kisses, the expert way he'd ravaged her, made her yearn for more.

'Have you changed your mind? Or do you wish for a dictionary to find the right words?'

She snapped herself free of the mesmerising, surely overblown, memory and struggled to focus. If she managed to prove her worth, maybe redeem herself a little in this room, she could begin to right the wrong she'd done.

'The previous treaty was skewed in favour of Valderra, we all know that. And yet Mendez never went through with it.'

'He didn't go through with it because the only copy of the Santo Sierran version, which had been witnessed by the King and legalised by each member of the council, went missing. To this day we do not know what happened to it.'

Jasmine's gaze snapped to Reyes.

The clear warning in his eyes stilled any words she'd been thinking of speaking. Fighting to keep her composure, she faced the council as Alvarez continued. 'And also because he's propelled by greed, but at the moment he holds all the cards.'

Jasmine shook her head. 'He holds all the cards because you choose to hide away in the dark.'

'Excuse me?' Reyes rasped.

An icy shiver raced across her skin but she persevered.

'Why don't you just call his bluff?'

'I won't gamble my kingdom's economic future on a bluff, Jasmine. If the choice were mine to make, I'd cut him off at the knees. But I can't do that. Not yet.'

The sound of her name on his lips produced another shiver. One that stalled her breath and made her lose her train of thought.

Jasmine frowned. 'So…what's the alternative?'

Silence descended on the table. The hairs on her nape stood up and Jasmine had a sense of foreboding so strong, she stumbled back and sank into her chair.

Reyes locked eyes with each member of his council before linking his fingers together. Poised, regal, his profile was so captivating, she couldn't have looked away if she'd tried. But she still knew she didn't want to hear what he was about to say.

'Unless another solution is forthcoming, or a new treaty is negotiated in the next few weeks, it seems my solution is to buy time by finding myself a bride.'

CHAPTER NINE

'BUT...THERE HAS to be another way!'

Reyes stared at Jasmine. Her lips were pressed together after her outburst.

'Miss Nichols—'

Reyes held up his hand to stop his second advisor. 'Go on,' he said to Jasmine. His curiosity was getting the better of him by the minute. If what she was proposing was better than the idea of marrying a faceless stranger in order to maintain peace, he was all for it.

His one attempt to marry had left harrowing scars that he would never forget. Until his sister, Isabella, had dissolved her engagement recently, Reyes had accepted that he would rule Santo Sierra in his lifetime, then let his sister's heirs inherit the throne.

But once again, the mantle was firmly on his shoulders.

'What if we can prove that he was behind the treaty going missing?'

Reyes surged to his feet, knocking the chair over. 'Gentlemen, give me the room.'

His men continued to stare at Jasmine with varying degrees of astonishment and suspicion. He slammed his hand on the table. 'Now!'

They scrambled up and hurried out.

'What the hell do you think you're doing?'

She jumped back at his bellow. 'I'm trying to help.'

He speared a hand through his hair. 'By putting yourself in the crosshairs of a dangerous man?' he demanded.

'But this is your council...'

'Some of whom are set in their ways and don't welcome

the sort of changes I hope to implement when I ascend to the throne.'

She frowned. 'And you think if they know…?' She stopped and gulped.

'Until I know who I can trust, I'm not prepared to take that risk with your life.' The knowledge that she'd almost given herself away greatly agitated him. He paced in front of her, trying to decipher why protecting her meant so much to him.

From the corner of his eye, he watched her reach out.

'Reyes—'

'No, don't defy me on this, Jasmine. I won't change my mind. I can't have another destroyed life on my conscience.' The words tumbled out.

They both froze. He saw the shock rocking through him reflected on her face.

'What…what do you mean?' Her voice was whisper-thin, puzzled.

He chopped off her question with a flick of his hand. 'It doesn't matter.' He took a deep breath to regain the balance he seemed to lose so easily around her. 'I'm calling the council back. You'll refrain from mentioning what happened in Rio. Am I clear?'

For the first time since he'd known her, she nodded readily.

He strode to the door, shock still rocking his system. His men came back. They tossed ideas around half-heartedly, until he clenched his fist.

'Gentlemen, we need to discuss the subject of my bride.'

Jasmine made a rough noise of disagreement. He ignored her. Looking at her would remind him of what he'd let slip. Remind him how easily she got under his skin.

'Well, in a way your current trade visits are a good way of introducing any prospective brides to the people. But…' Alvarez cleared his throat '…you need to be a little less closed off, Your Highness.'

'Excuse me?'

'I think any further visits should be less clandestine. The

people need to see their prince embracing life a little. Remind them that you're flesh and blood, and not a fairy-tale figure locked away in an ivory tower.'

Reyes pinched the bridge of his nose. 'Are you saying my discretion is a flaw?'

'I'm saying the people don't really know you. You brought Santo Sierra right up to the treaty table after your father fell ill, but the fact remains that the finish line was never crossed. And Santo Sierrans aren't quite sure how to take that. You don't want to estrange yourself from the people.'

Fury bubbled beneath his skin. Beside him, Jasmine's tension slammed into him. Her face was clouded with a mixture of displeasure and misery. When her eyes met his, he glimpsed regret in them.

'So you're saying whatever I do, the people won't be satisfied until they have me pressing the flesh, kissing babies with a promise of a royal wedding and an heir to swoon over?' Reyes couldn't suppress his sneer. The thought of putting himself out there, to be prodded and gawped over by the media, turned his stomach.

Alvarez knew Reyes's personal history and how he felt about the media. But his councillor nodded warily. 'That would be one way to reassure the people, yes.'

Gathering his fraying control, he turned back to his men. 'And there's no chance of presenting them with a royal wedding via Isabella?' He tried for one last ounce of a reprieve. 'Perhaps we can still rescue the situation with her ex-betrothed if we move fast enough...'

He stopped when Costanzo shook his head. 'Her fiancé declared he didn't want anything to do with Her Highness any longer after she broke things off. We had to pay his family reparations for the cancelled engagement. They won't reconsider Her Highness as a suitor.'

'Dios!' He looked at Jasmine, his blood boiling.

That look was still on her face—worry, regret. He looked

past that. To the luscious mouth that was parted slightly as her chest rose and fell in shallow breaths.

He wanted to forget that she was responsible for all this. Forget that the more he spoke to her, the more he doubted that her character was as black as he'd first thought. Reyes just wanted to forget. And in that moment, he wanted to use the most elemental way possible to achieve oblivion.

Her.

That stirring grew until his whole body thrummed with a carnal demand he couldn't deny.

What was wrong with him?

His youngest advisor cleared his throat. 'If Your Highness prefers, we can pursue this as a short-term union. Only until the economic situation in the kingdom stabilises.' He tapped a few keys on his tablet.

Reyes drummed his fingers on the table as he waited.

Finally, the advisor looked up. 'And I think Miss Nichols may be right. She's suitably placed to help.'

'She hasn't brought up any new solutions to Santo Sierra's problems that we haven't already considered.'

'No, but she could be the right person to broker a temporary marriage for you.'

'Excuse me?'

Reyes's eyes narrowed at her outraged tone.

His advisor glanced at her, then back at his tablet. 'According to the information I have here, you brokered the marriage between a US senator and his mistress once you arranged a discreet divorce from his wife of thirty years.'

Jasmine's mouth dropped open. 'That's supposed to be confidential.'

A douse of cold water cooled Reyes's raging temperature. 'Seems there's no end to your dubious talent,' he murmured.

Her face flushed. 'I wasn't responsible for him leaving his wife, nor was I responsible for finding the mistress, if that's what you're implying. I only assisted with the financial arrangements and ensured each party walked away happy.'

Her gaze swung to the men at the end of the table. How was it possible that one look from her commanded their silence? Reyes watched, intrigued, as she crossed her arms and narrowed her eyes for emphasis.

'That's not what you're asking me to do, surely? For what you need for Re…His Highness, you require an elite professional matchmaker. That's not what I specialise in. When I said I'd help I meant with the *economic* issues facing the kingdom.'

'This is an issue facing the kingdom. And one that has to be addressed sooner rather than later. With Isabella's marriage off the table, we need to give the people something to sustain their faith,' Alvarez said.

Pressure built at Reyes's temple. He wanted to deny what his council were saying. But deep down he couldn't dismiss that his people needed a healthy dose of bolstering news. Reyes had dashed their hopes of a royal wedding once before, five years ago, when he'd thrown Anaïs out of his life.

With his mother's subsequent death four years ago behind the wheel of her lover's car, and his father's illness soon afterwards, the only good news the Santo Sierran people had been given was the signing of the treaty and Isabella's wedding.

Both had failed to materialise. In the meantime, Mendez was pushing his greedy fingers into Santo Sierran affairs. It needed to end.

But marriage…

The only template he'd witnessed had been one mired in deception, misery and acrimony. It wasn't something he wanted to reproduce. If he was to take this road, it needed to be permanent. With both sides clear in their role and with no room for misunderstanding.

He looked down the table. Clenching his jaw, he nodded. 'The marriage will be a permanent one, not a short-term try-it-and-see-what-happens. My life isn't a scripted reality show to peddle to the people.'

Costanzo beamed with pleasure. 'Of course, Your Highness. That's a very wise decision. We'll set the ball rolling straight away—'

Reyes held up his hand. 'No, we'll reconvene in three days.'

The smile turned into a frown. 'But, Your Highness—'

'Arrange for the royal press secretary to include an addendum to my Paris itinerary. They can sell it as an investment-stroke-leisure trip.' He turned to Jasmine, noting that she'd gone pale again. 'Miss Nichols will be responsible for finding me five suitable candidates. Fly them to Paris for interviews after my investment meetings.'

'You're going ahead with it?' Her face was deliberately blank, but her eyes were pools of shock.

Somehow that bothered him. He shook himself out of the curious feeling. 'For my people's sake, yes.'

She drew in a shaky breath and looked down at her linked hands.

He surged to his feet, not liking the feeling that he'd been judged and found guilty. Nor did he like the sensation of a noose closing around his neck.

'Three days, gentlemen.'

'Yes, Your Highness.

In that moment, Reyes hated his title. Hated the responsibility weighing down on his shoulders. But despite the mixed emotions, there was one solemn vow he couldn't deny. He owed his people a better life than they'd enjoyed so far. And he intended to do whatever it took to make right his mistakes.

'You know you could've been done with me much quicker if you'd told them.' Questions had been swirling in her mind since Reyes's councilmen had left hours ago. But the one she'd wanted to ask wouldn't form, so she was trying a different route.

Reyes turned from the view to stare at her. 'Told them what?'

'What my role was in…'

'The treaty's disappearance?'

Jasmine jerked her head, still surprised he'd joined her for dinner and even more so that he'd stayed after they'd shared a delicious Spanish tapas meal on the terrace. Although the meal had gone by in near total silence, she couldn't help but feel a little less apprehensive of her fate.

She cradled the as yet untouched glass of red wine in her hands, watching the sun set on the horizon. Trying not to stare at Reyes Navarre's stunning profile as he leaned against the large pillar, facing the garden.

'Because if I had you'd be on your way to a maximum security prison in Santo Sierra. Your crime would be condemned as treason in my kingdom.'

Her heart stopped and her palms grew clammy. 'Aren't I headed there anyway? Something about getting a permanent tan?'

'Perhaps. But you might want to do something about delaying your arrival there. Before I came to Rio, I was in the process of enforcing a law that prohibited male and female prisoners being housed in the same penitentiary. That law hasn't passed yet.'

She inhaled sharply. 'You mean men and women are kept in the same prison?'

He shrugged. 'The old council deemed all criminals to be worthless regardless of their gender.'

Ice cascaded down her spine. 'But…that's barbaric!'

'They didn't care that they were potentially turning criminals who could be rehabilitated into irredeemable monsters. So do you regret my silence on your behalf?'

She slowly shook her head. 'No, I don't.' Her eyes met his. Whatever he saw in hers made him lift an eyebrow. Jasmine looked away quickly. 'I… Thank you.'

His mouth compressed. 'I neither want nor accept your gratitude. Retribution is still coming your way, one way or the other.'

The warning sent further chills dancing over her skin. While a part of her wanted him to spell out her fate and get her punishment over and done with, another part of her wanted to plead with him for mercy. She'd wronged him. Wronged his country. And he'd still saved her, albeit temporarily, from whatever the consequences were for her acts.

Reminding herself that this was the man who was contemplating marrying to please his people, she took a fortifying breath.

'My stepfather was kidnapped.'

His head whipped towards her. 'Excuse me?'

'First he was blackmailed through me, then kidnapped. He has…or had a gambling problem. He's been battling with it for almost twenty years. He embezzled government funds. And I'm not talking pennies. It was serious money. Getting caught would've meant a long prison sentence for him. So he borrowed money from a loan shark.'

'Who then turned the tables on him and demanded even more?'

She nodded. 'He said unless I brought him the treaty, he would harm my stepfather.'

Chilled grey eyes narrowed. 'Who was the loan shark?'

'His name was Joaquin Esteban. I don't know whether that's his real name or not—'

'Don't worry, I'll find him. So he took your stepfather?' he asked.

She nodded. 'In the middle of the night, right in front of my mother. They roughed him up. Broke his arm.' She shivered and he straightened from the wall.

'Did they hurt you?' His was voice was grave, intense.

'No. It happened when I was…with you, on your boat.'

His eyes narrowed. 'I don't recall you receiving a call.'

'You were asleep. My mother called. She was beside herself. I didn't want to do it, Reyes, please believe me, but I couldn't leave him in the hands of those men.'

If she'd expected sympathy, she was to be sorely disappointed. But for a heartbeat, his expression altered. Softened a touch.

'So where is this moralistic gambler of a stepfather, then? Still in his comfy government position?'

Irritation snapped along her nerves. 'Yes. But he's seeking help.'

'How noble of him.'

'He doesn't know what I did. He suspects but I don't want him to know. He'll be devastated. We can't all be perfect role models. Some of us try to put unfortunate deeds behind us and seek better lives.'

'And some of you fail miserably at it.'

Turning sideways, she set her glass down on the table. 'You have a right to condemn me. Believe me, I've condemned myself countless times. But I wanted you to understand why I did what I did. Obviously I was wasting my breath.'

Reyes twirled his wine glass, one broad shoulder still leaning against the white pillar. Dressed in a white shirt and casual trousers, he looked sinfully breathtaking. Until she glimpsed the shadows in his eyes.

Her heart lurched as his words once again swirled in her mind. *I can't have another destroyed life on my conscience.*

Her eyes rose back to his face. He was watching her with that incisive look that seemed to see right into her soul. He took a slow sip, savouring the wine before swallowing.

'Contain your righteous indignation. You'll have to fall on your sword a hell of a lot more times before you breach the surface of my mercy. But I have a few minutes to spare, so please…carry on.'

She sighed. 'I'm sorry. I never intended for you to…for anyone to suffer for what I did.' Her gaze dropped to his midriff. His mouth tightened. 'If you could find it in your heart—'

His mocking laughter stopped her painful pleas. 'My *heart*?'

She gripped the edge of the table. 'I don't see the funny side to what I just said.'

'My heart is the last organ you should be attempting to appease.'

'I don't... I'm afraid you've lost me.'

His smile held that hint of sadness she'd glimpsed at their first meeting in Rio. 'You'd be wasting your time trying to appeal to something that doesn't exist.'

CHAPTER TEN

JASMINE STARED AT HIM, trying to work out if he was mocking her or not. He wasn't. That bleak look was deepening and his breathing was growing shallow and choppy as if he was caught in a distressing memory.

Before she could stop herself, she reached out and touched his arm.

He flinched. Brows clamped together, he stared down at her. 'What are you doing?'

'You seem a little...lost.'

One corner of his mouth lifted. 'And you thought you'd rescue me?' he bit out.

'Yes. Obviously, I was wrong to do so.' She turned away, unable to stomach the wildly volatile moods she experienced around this man. One minute she wanted to hurt him for his mockery, the next she wanted to ease whatever emotional pain haunted him.

And it was clear he was suffering. As for his reference to his non-existent heart, the lengths he was willing to go to for his people proved otherwise.

'You were talking about your stepfather?'

She frowned. 'I'm not sure that I want to any more.'

'Because I'm not whimpering with sympathy?'

'Because you pretend you're devoid of empathy, but I know that's not true.'

'Your dubious powers of deduction at work again?'

She perched on the edge of the table and folded her arms before the temptation to touch him spiralled out of control. Far from being cold as he tried to portray, Reyes was warm, passionate.

Any woman would be lucky to have him as her husband...

Her thoughts screeched to a halt. The stone that had lodged itself in her belly since his announcement in his study grew larger.

Which was ludicrous. All they'd shared was a one-night stand. An incredible one for her, but a brief, meaningless one nonetheless.

She had no right to experience this ongoing bewildering pain in her heart when she thought of what he planned to do. And the idea that he wasn't looking to marry for the short term, but for ever, shouldn't make her world darken with despair.

She had no claim on Reyes...

Jasmine started when he lifted his glass and abruptly drained his wine. She jerked upright when he lifted an imperious hand and summoned a guard, who'd been somewhere tucked out of her sight.

'What are you doing?'

'Since you're unwilling to carry on even the semblance of conversation, I'm having you escorted to your suite. We'll meet at noon tomorrow and you'll present me with a list of suitable candidates.'

Her fingers curled around the edge of the table at the thought of the task she'd been set. She wanted to refuse; wanted to tell him she'd rather rot in jail than help him find the next woman to warm his bed.

But how could she go back on her word to do whatever was needed to right her wrong?

One of his bodyguards approached. He wasn't the one who'd accosted her in the gardens this morning. In fact, from being a constant shadow, that other guard seemed to have disappeared.

This guard nodded at whatever Reyes was saying to him.

'Wait!'

Reyes lifted a bored brow at her.

'It's still early.' At his continued indolent look, she pursed her lips. 'Fine, I'll talk. My stepfather is perfect in every sense, except when it comes to his gambling.'

She looked from Reyes to the bodyguard. After several

heartbeats, Reyes dismissed the guard with a sharp nod. Walking past where she remained perched, he grabbed the half-finished bottle of wine, frowned at her untouched glass and refilled his own. He sat down, crossing his legs, so his thighs were dangerously close to her knee.

Jasmine pulled stronger on her runaway composure. 'He's a kind, gentle man and he cares deeply for my mother.'

A look passed through his eyes, but was gone before she could work out what it meant.

'Where does your biological father fit into this scenario?'

His voice lacked mockery, a fact for which she was thankful. 'He left when I was barely out of nappies. And he was the first in a long line of "fathers",' she quoted, 'who came and went before I was a teenager.'

Reyes sipped his wine. Said nothing.

'I know what you're thinking,' she ventured when the silence stretched.

His eyes gleamed. 'I sincerely doubt that.'

She shrugged. 'Well, whether you're thinking it or not, my past shaped me. I was angry with the world and with a mother who couldn't see how hopeless the men she dated were. By the time my stepfather came along, I was...in a bad way.'

'How bad?'

Jasmine didn't want to tell him. Didn't want to see the contempt in his eyes, or relive the bleakest point in her life. She'd been there, done that, and wore the shame underneath her skin and physical scars on her body.

She didn't want to go there, but Reyes's steady gaze demanded an answer.

'A spell in juvenile detention when I was sixteen,' she found herself confessing.

He froze. *'Dios...'* he murmured.

Thick mortification crept over her. Struggling to cover it, she laughed. 'Now you know my deepest, darkest secret. I'm guessing you'll be holding this over my head, too—'

'Stop talking, Jasmine.'

She clamped her mouth shut. He watched her with a curious expression, his gaze intensely assessing.

'How long were you in detention?'

Strangely she couldn't read any judgement in his tone. She reminded herself that as a prince he was skilled in hiding his true emotion. But then, he hadn't held back so far—

'Answer me,' he bit out roughly.

'Nine months.'

'What for?'

She grimaced. 'I *accidentally* set fire to a drug dealer's warehouse.'

'Is that experience why you found the handcuffs distressing?'

'You mean there are people who love being handcuffed?' she threw back.

One brow spiked.

Heat stained her cheeks. 'Yes, well, I didn't like it at the time. Still don't. Those days were the most traumatic of my life. Please don't force me to relive them.'

He put his glass down and leaned forward, elbows on his knees. His intensity increased a thousandfold. As did the intoxicating scent of his aftershave and warm skin. Jasmine clenched her thighs to keep from moving closer.

'What happened after you were released?'

'My stepfather. And yes, it may sound like a fairy tale, but he saved us. And even with his flaws, he turned out to be better than any man out there, even the man whose blood runs through my veins.'

Grey eyes snagged hers. Still no condemnation in them, just a stark curiosity.

'But the gambling became a problem, obviously,' he said.

She nodded. 'He was married before, but his wife died. That's when the problem escalated for him. He stopped for a while when he and my mother were dating, but after they married he started again. No matter how much we tried, we couldn't convince him to give it up. It made me sad. I know it worried him, too, that he couldn't beat it. But I couldn't condemn him. No matter what, he was the best father I knew. When Joaquin sank his claws into him, I had no choice. I couldn't let Stephen suffer.'

'Where was your mother in all of this?' The question was framed so tersely, with a bitter underlay that grazed sharply over her senses.

She looked at him. Whatever emotion he was holding had triggered tension in his body, like a predator ready to unleash its base nature should its prey fall within his grasp. Despite her nape tingling in warning, she wanted to move closer, experience that overwhelming danger.

Clearing her throat, she answered, 'My mother is what a psychologist would term wilfully blind. She means the world to me, but doesn't see what's right in front of her. Or she chooses to ignore it in favour of burying her head in the sand.'

The misery that her mother's attitude to life had brought her before Stephen had fallen in love with her had been a stark warning for Jasmine not to travel down the same path. She understood her mother better now, but it didn't make the pain of her late teens go away.

She glanced at Reyes and saw grudging understanding. But the look was wiped clean a moment later.

'Understanding the motive doesn't negate the crime.'

The unexpected surge of tears shocked Jasmine.

What was wrong with her? He'd told her he didn't have a heart. If she chose to disbelieve him, any hurt she felt was her own fault.

Blinking rapidly, she started to rise. 'No, but a little forgiveness goes a long way.'

He clamped a hand on her thigh.

Her heart took a dive, then picked itself up and banged hard against her ribs.

Reyes questioned his sanity. Except the voice was quickly smothered beneath the headier emotions swimming in his head.

His hand was halfway down her thigh, the soft cotton of her sundress crushing beneath his fingers. He moved his hand lower.

She gasped as they connected, skin to skin. Hers was soft, smooth like the fur of his sister's pet cat. And as with Sheba's pelt, he wanted to keep on stroking her.

He watched her struggle, knew the emotions she fought were the same as the ones he battled with. The chemistry that had gripped them the first time he'd set eyes on her flared high, spiking through his blood until he didn't bother to deny its existence any longer.

'You dislike me for stating the truth?'

'I dislike the brutality of it. And the complete absence of sympathy.'

Knowing he'd done a good job of hiding his feelings should've pleased Reyes. If his feelings weren't apparent, they couldn't be manipulated, used against him. So why did the thought that he'd succeeded send a pulse of discontentment through him? Why did he want to wipe that hurt look from her face? 'I warned you not to search for feelings that don't exist—'

'And I told you I don't believe that emotion doesn't exist inside you.'

He surged to his feet. 'I've never met anyone like you,' he said, not sure whether his agitation stemmed from the Tempranillo he'd consumed or the fact that she challenged him at every turn where no else dared to.

She sucked in a breath and her eyes stayed on his. Daring. Searching. Apprehensive. 'Nor I you. So this should be fun.'

A reluctant smile tugged at his lips. *Fun*...

Another word he'd associated with her that first time. A word he hadn't let into his life for a very long time.

He started to draw back from the brink of whatever fever gripped him.

She stepped closer. Her hands slid around his waist, holding him in place.

Again her daring floored him...excited him. The women

he'd dated in his distant past had been either too overawed with his status to show much spine, or had been so eager to prove they were worthy of his time, they'd overreached. Either way, he'd tended to lose interest long before they were done in the bedroom.

Jasmine Nichols made his senses jump without uttering a word. And when she did speak, he found himself held rapt.

In the last hour, the woman she'd revealed herself to be intrigued him even more. She'd experienced adversity of the worst kind, and come through it.

And with her hand on him and her parted lips so close, all he could see, smell, *anticipate*, was her.

Drawn into a web he couldn't shake, he angled his head. 'I don't do fun, Jasmine.'

Her back arched, bringing her closer. Her mouth brushed his. He jerked at the zap of electricity. Her hands tightened around him. 'Sure you do. You just don't like to admit it.'

The sound that rumbled from inside him emerged harsh and bewildered. *'Dios...'*

He spiked his hand through her hair and kissed her. Hard. Roughly.

He palmed her breasts, gloried in their fullness, and swallowed her jagged gasp of pleasure when his thumb grazed her nipple. The sight and taste of them flashed through his mind. He squeezed the bud. Harder. She made a rougher sound. More demanding. More receptive.

His blood thrummed faster.

Capturing her waist, he pulled her into his body. Her hands drifted up from his torso, up to his shoulders. Every nerve yearned for closer contact. The ultimate contact.

He was fast reaching the point where he would be unable to deny the need to take, the need to reprise the headiness of their encounter in Rio.

Her mouth parted wider, her tongue caressing his. Reyes drove in, tasting her with deep, hungry kisses that robbed them both of breath.

His erection throbbed. Demanded satisfaction.

Dios, this was crazy. Making the same mistake twice was unconscionable. He needed to pull back.

But he couldn't. His thumb angled her jaw and he claimed another kiss. He didn't realise he'd bent her backwards until her elbows propped on the table to support herself.

Needing to breathe, he took a beat. Looked at her, spread before him like a banquet.

A tempting, *forbidden* banquet. He'd given in once and the resulting chaos still echoed through his life. Perhaps he understood her motivations a little now. Perhaps he would even contemplate forgiveness at some distant point in the future.

But he couldn't revisit the eye of the storm.

Sucking in a deep breath, he stepped back, smashing down on his body's insistence that he finish what he'd started.

He denied his body, denied his mind. It would've been easy to take what he wanted; what he craved. But he knew it would come at a price. A price he couldn't afford to pay.

CHAPTER ELEVEN

'So, JUST SO we're clear, you want me to enquire whether she's a good kisser, or should I go the whole hog and ask her if she's dynamite in bed, too?' Jasmine folded her arms and drummed her fingers against her elbows.

She knew her foul mood stemmed from the tossing and turning she'd done last night. And her triple vomiting session this morning. She knew *why* she'd tossed and turned. Just as she feared her suspicions on why she was throwing up would be confirmed, as soon as she found a way to visit a chemist. She wasn't afraid to admit she was terrified of what the results of a pregnancy test would show. And not just for herself. She'd already thrown Reyes's world into chaos once. How would he react *if* it turned out she was carrying his child?

She'd debated through the night whether to tell him of her suspicions, and had elected to wait. There was no point stirring the hornet's nest even harder until she had concrete proof.

Feeling weak and more than a little apprehensive of what fate held in store for her, she'd have given her right arm not to perform the task of finding Reyes Navarre a bride.

He leaned back in his chair, his gaze coolly assessing. 'The latter qualities I will discover for myself long before our wedding night. Once you've tackled the more important characteristics of loyalty, trust and dependability, of course.'

'I'd never consider anyone who didn't possess those qualities. But how on earth am I supposed to know whether she's a good kisser or not?'

His eyebrow quirked and she had a feeling he was toying with her. 'Aren't you supposed to be good at your job?'

'Brokering deals and calming anxious parties before multinational mergers, yes. Judging whether a woman is a good kisser based on her pedigree, not so much.'

'So you're admitting failure before you've even started?' he asked.

She looked away, afraid he'd see the depth of the anguish she couldn't will away, no matter how much she tried. 'I'm not afraid to admit I'm not the right person for this job. We slept together, Reyes—' she saw him tense, but she forced herself to continue '—and despite everything that happened afterwards, it wasn't a casual thing for me. I can't just brush it off…' She stopped before she dug herself into a hole she'd never be able to emerge from.

'Are you saying you can't stay objective in this task?'

She forced herself to meet his gaze. 'I'm saying I have feelings. I'll do it if you want me to but I don't have to like it.'

A look crossed his face, but his expression shuttered before she could read it. 'Understood.'

Jasmine forced herself to glance down at the shortlist she'd compiled at four a.m. when she'd finally conceded sleep was a pipe dream. She rattled off the names, watching his face for a reaction. His features remained blank.

'I'm going to call their representatives. Arrange for us to meet them in Paris next week. Shall I arrange to send your private jet for them or do you want them to fly commercial?'

'I don't micromanage. Liaise with my head of security on modes of transport. And we're not flying to Paris next week. We're leaving tomorrow, and then on to Santo Sierra at the end of the week.' He slid his chair closer to his desk and opened a file.

'What?' Her heart thumped harder with a mixture of desolation and anxiety. 'I'm good at my job, but I can't find you a bride in twenty-four hours, *Your Highness*.' Pressure built in her head with the knowledge that she needed to find out once and for all whether she carried his child.

'Have you seen the news today?' he enquired.

'No. Should I have?'

His fists tightened on the desk for a moment before he relaxed. 'There was a riot in San Domenica last night.'

'Santo Sierra's capital?'

He nodded. 'Several people were hurt, including women and children, in the main square. Thankfully, no one was killed. My people are growing restless. Their anxiety is being fuelled, no doubt by Mendez's people. I have to return soon or things will get worse.'

The throb of worry in his voice was unmistakeable. For the first time she accepted that his councillors were right. Santo Sierra needed a good news story to bolster the people's confidence in its monarchy.

Caught in the quandary of having her feelings ravaged in the process of finding Reyes a wife, while suspecting she was carrying his child, and doing what she could to fix the damage she'd caused, Jasmine took a deep breath and gathered her composure.

'I'll make sure the candidates are in Paris for when we arrive.' She picked up her tablet and headed for the door.

'Jasmine?'

Her heart stuttered at the use of her first name.

'Yes?' Her answer emerged shakier than she would've wished.

'Cross Petra Nikolova off your list. We dated briefly once. She's been known to take certain banned substances on occasion. The last thing I intend to foist on my subjects is a drug-dabbling queen. And you can also delete Sienna Hamilton.'

Every single good intention fled out of her head. Her anxiety ramped up, along with a buzzing in her head and a sick feeling in her stomach she shockingly diagnosed as writhing jealousy. Coupled with the suspected extra hormones raging through her body, Jasmine had to lock her knees and count to ten before she could speak.

'What's wrong with Miss Hamilton?' Her voice trembled in a way she detested.

When his eyes locked on hers, his expression was far from mocking. 'She's a serial cheater. She's discreet about it, but I prefer not to wonder in who else's bed my wife has been when I return home at night.'

She stared at him, dying to ask why pain clouded his eyes when he talked about adultery. But, unwilling to drive the knife that seemed to be wedged in her chest further, she wiped the question from her mind. Realising she hadn't taken a breath since Reyes mentioned kissing other women, Jasmine forced herself to breathe.

'You realise that leaves me with just three candidates?' she said around the knot in her throat. It was three more than she wanted to deal with, but she couldn't see any way around this harrowing task.

He cracked a hard, sad smile. 'Then you need to make doubly sure they are right for the job.' His tone said she was dismissed.

Which was good because Jasmine couldn't get out of there fast enough. Except she couldn't leave just yet.

Reyes raised his head when she retraced her steps to his desk. 'Can I help you with something else?'

'I need to go into town this morning.'

He frowned. 'Why?'

Because I need to know whether my life is about to change for ever.

'I need stuff.'

He looked down his nose at her. Waited.

A blush warmed her cheeks. 'Women's stuff.'

Her tiny hope for him to feel a little bit of her embarrassment died a quick death when he returned his attention to his papers.

'Reyes? Can I get one of your men to drive me into town?'

'No,' he replied.

'Come on—'

'I'll drive you myself. We'll go after lunch.'

No, no, no!

* * *

Entering the solarium, she sank into the nearest lounger, clenched her fingers around the tablet to stop them shaking.

She tried to reason with herself. The likelihood that a crown prince would be caught shopping for feminine products in a chemist was very minimal.

But then so had the likelihood of her ending up in his bed in Rio. The odds that she could be pregnant with Reyes's child were one in a million, but she knew to her cost that fate was vested in singling her out for her parlour tricks.

She could be worrying over nothing. The tenderness in her breasts could be the result of her imagination. Or the residual effect of Reyes caressing them last night…

She forced herself to look at the list of candidates she needed to contact…and flung the tablet away. Covering her face with her hands, she caught a low moan before it escaped.

What was wrong with her? One night of sex and one heavy-kissing session with Reyes Navarre and she couldn't handle the idea of him with another woman? No, she couldn't deny that her feelings were more to do with the fact that she might be carrying his baby. And the growing sense that she couldn't stand the thought of him being married to someone else whether his child was growing inside her or not.

Would Reyes go ahead with marrying someone else if she was carrying his child, or would he consider another option? Like her…

Hope rose up inside her. She pushed it away.

She was going crazy…

He would never consider her in a million years. Her heart lurched. Shaking her head, she focused on the names.

One young duchess. One daughter of a media mogul. One self-made millionaire with an extensive philanthropic background.

On paper any one of the remaining three could be crown princess material and would no doubt do whatever it took to secure the attention, if not the heart, of a man like Reyes Navarre.

So get a move on...

The quicker she got this over with, the quicker she could return to her life. Forget all about Reyes and the feel of his mouth on hers, his strong arms around her.

By the time Reyes strode into the solarium, Jasmine had secured the enthusiastic agreement of all three and had arranged for their travel to Paris.

'Something's come up. I can't take you into town. Make a list of what you need. I'll have Carmelita get them for you.'

Her stomach lurched in a queasy roll. Having Reyes find out what she suspected before she knew for sure was out of the question. 'Umm...I'd rather get them myself. If you're busy, it can wait till we get to Paris.'

He frowned, but nodded and walked away.

Jasmine wasn't proud of taking the coward's way out, buying herself some more time before she had to face whatever fate had in store for her. So when the tears stung her eyes, she raced up the stairs to her room and let them fall.

'You'll be dining with the duchess at the Paris Ultime this evening at eight. I've reserved a private dining room for you and once you review the menu I can provide it to the private chef who'll be catering for you. The duchess is allergic to shellfish. Oh, and she doesn't eat carbs after six, so she requests that a bread basket not be served. She can't resist the temptation, apparently.' Jasmine made her voice crisp, businesslike, so the pain of the vice tightening around her heart wouldn't bleed through her voice.

Reyes raised an eyebrow at her as their limo left the private airport and drove towards the French capital.

'You think it's a good sign that the woman who's to bring hope to my people can't resist a simple bread basket?'

Jasmine shrugged. 'We all have our faults. If hers is a simple carbs issue, then you're all set.' She tried to keep her voice light, but the stone wedged in her belly made even thought difficult.

The last thing she wanted to discuss was the eating habits of Reyes's future queen.

'Do you resist bread baskets after six, Jasmine?'

God, why couldn't she stop her heart from flipping over each time he said her name like that? 'Nope. Bread is a vice I happily embrace.'

The moment the words were out of her mouth, she regretted it. A chill permeated the atmosphere. Reyes stared at her, tight jawed. Jasmine wondered whether to apologise, but then dismissed it. She'd apologised enough. She was here, making amends. Even if it involved doing a job every fibre of her being rejected.

After several minutes, she cleared her throat. 'Liliana Simpson will have lunch with you tomorrow, and I've scheduled Berenice Holden for an early dinner. Once you make your decision, I'll liaise with your royal press secretary about making an announcement. I've also arranged for a few photographers to take some pictures...' She stopped when his jaw clenched harder. 'What?'

'One camera, one photograph, one photographer.' His tone was acid.

'But I thought you wanted the world to see that you're alive and dating? You can't hide away for ever. You need to get in front of the people. Show them that you care about them. That you're excited to lead them. And that you're also not a eunuch.'

'Excuse me?'

She attempted a shrug that fell short of the mark. 'One photograph isn't going to do the job.'

'You forget there was a riot in my kingdom less than twenty-four hours ago. I can't be seen living it up in Paris, proving my manhood, while my people are suffering. The article will stress heavily that I'm on my way home, possibly with a potential bride in tow. The intention is to take their minds off their anxiety without making it seem like I've forgotten about them, is it not?'

'Yes, of course. I'll take care of it.'

As she made unnecessary notes in her tablet her mind raced. She could feel the waves of tension coming off his body, and knew Reyes would rather be in Santo Sierra, seeing to his people, than here in Paris vetting potential brides.

While the thought perplexingly lifted her heart, she couldn't help but be concerned for him.

'Have you thought about what you'll do about Mendez?' she asked.

His mouth compressed. Wedging his elbow on the armrest, he glanced at her. 'Once the wedding is done and I've elected a new council, I'll make him a take-it-or-leave-it offer. The time for pandering to his whim is over.'

She nodded. When he turned to look out of the window, she stared at his profile. The question she'd been avoiding hovered on the tip of her tongue.

'Can I ask you a question?' she blurted.

Grey eyes narrowed on her. 'Go ahead.'

'Why are there no pictures of you taken since your mother died?'

A chilled look entered his eyes. 'Because I don't court publicity. Not like...' He stopped and exhaled harshly.

Her heart clenched at the bleakness in his eyes. 'Like your mother? I know she liked to...that she was a media darling.'

'Less of a darling, more of a whore,' he countered mercilessly.

Jasmine flinched. 'I'm sorry.'

'Why? We finally have something in common. Mothers who would've been better off remaining childless.'

'I wouldn't go as far as that. After all, if that had happened, neither you or I would be here.'

His gaze raked her face, as if he were trying to burrow under her skin, see inside her soul again. 'And our night in Rio would never have happened,' he murmured.

Her breath stalled. 'No...I guess not.'

'Do you regret that, Jasmine?' he rasped.

'I like it when you call me Jasmine. Miss Nichols makes me sound like a kindergarten teacher.'

A low, deep laugh broke from his lips, but he continued to stare at her. Then he lifted his hand and traced a finger down her cheek. 'You haven't answered my question, Jasmine.'

'Do I regret Rio?' The truth wasn't difficult to admit. But she feared the can of worms she would be opening by admitting it, even to herself. She licked her dry bottom lip. 'The first part, not at all. It was the most memorable night of my life.'

His eyes darkened and his nostrils flared. 'And the second part?' he demanded.

'The second part...very, very much. I would do anything to take it back.'

He said nothing, but he nodded after several seconds. And she dared to hope that he believed her.

CHAPTER TWELVE

THE DINNER JACKET he wore felt tight, restrictive. And someone had turned up the temperature in the private dining room. Or had it been turned down?

Dios...

Reyes passed a finger underneath his collar and moved the food around on his plate.

'I would need to fly to Europe at least twice a month. I have a standing appointment for full works at my favourite spa in Switzerland.' Carefully styled blond hair curtained to one side as the duchess tilted her head. 'That won't be a problem, will it?'

The bread basket. Suddenly, Reyes needed it more than he needed to breathe.

'Reyes...you don't mind me calling you Reyes, do you? Or do you prefer Rey?' She smiled.

Perfect teeth. Perfect hair. Perfect manicure.

No character-forming scars on her body. As Jasmine had across her palm. Or that thin two-inch scar on her shoulder.

He growled under his breath. He was sitting opposite a beautiful, poised woman who was warm enough for his people to fall in love with. Visually, the duchess was the antithesis of his mother and Anaïs, and that alone would sway his people, who'd hated Queen Isolde Navarre, towards her.

And yet he couldn't stop thinking about the reluctant thief with the body that called to his like a siren to a sailor.

He forced himself to focus on his dinner companion. After another minute, he threw down his napkin, stood and smiled down at the duchess.

'We won't need to worry about what you'll call me. After tonight we'll most likely never meet again.'

He entered his suite twenty minutes later. It was barely nine o'clock so he knew Jasmine would still be up. He told himself he was searching for her to give her a piece of his mind about how appallingly his evening had gone.

He had a right to, after all.

When the living room proved empty, he contemplated leaving the dressing-down till morning. Going to the bar, he poured himself a cognac and walked out onto the penthouse terrace.

He heard the splash of her swimming before he rounded the corner to where the private pool was located.

Despite warning himself that he needed to stay away, he couldn't stop his feet propelling him forward until he was standing on the edge of the aqua-tiled pool, staring at her stunning figure as she swam underwater.

Her arms and legs kicked in a graceful flow, the sight of her scantily clad figure robbing him of breath and sanity. That feeling of skating on the edge of his control escalated to the point where he was in a foul mood by the time she broke the surface.

'You failed.' His snarl was deep and ruthless enough to make him inwardly grimace.

Nevertheless, he felt a measure of cheap satisfaction when she whirled to face him. 'Actually, I was winning. Twenty laps without stopping is an achievement for me.'

'I don't mean your swim. I mean you failed with the duchess.'

A single frown line marred her perfect skin. 'Okay. I guess that's why you're back early? What happened?'

Her legs continued to swirl lazily underwater as she stared up at him. Reyes's groin pounded hard as he followed the sexy movement.

When she raised her eyebrows, he dragged his gaze away, tried to find words to enumerate the duchess's faults. None came to mind. 'She lacked the qualities I need.'

Jasmine's eyes shadowed. She glanced away, then back at him. 'You did the kissing test?' An odd note in her voice made something jerk in his chest. He didn't have time to examine it because she kicked away from the edge. Her breasts bounced, and he nearly swallowed his tongue as flames spiked into his groin.

'I didn't need to. I knew she would fail.'

'Wow, you're psychic now?' Her tone had returned to normal. She swam towards the steps.

He followed, mesmerised by the curve of her spine and the roundness of her behind. He watched her rise from the pool and pluck a towel from the chair. His fingers tightened around his glass when she patted the towel over her body.

Focus! 'Perhaps you need to be reminded of my earlier statement. You *failed.*'

'You have two more candidates. Maybe you'll strike it lucky second time round. If not, three times will be the charm.'

The restlessness that prowled through him intensified. 'You'll come with me tomorrow.'

She froze and stared at him with wide, wounded eyes. 'I'd rather not, Reyes. I'm not the one marrying these women!'

He exhaled harshly. Ploughing a hand through his hair, he glared at her. 'I…need you.'

Her eyes widened further. He kicked himself for uttering words he had no business saying. 'No, you don't. I've done my bit. It's time to do yours.'

'*Dios!* Have you always been this infuriating?'

Her face fell. 'You think I'm infuriating?'

Reyes was overcome with a desire to placate her. Take that look off her face. Replace it with one of those stunning smiles that lit up his insides.

He pondered the feeling, adding extreme puzzlement to the many emotions he felt around this woman.

This woman should be in jail somewhere dark and harrowing, not enjoying the luxury of a Parisian emperor suite, wearing a sexy bikini, and swimming in his pool.

'Yes. You're infuriating. And you're also supposed to be good at your job. So far you're doing a pathetically poor attempt. Were you in my permanent employ I'd have fired you a long time ago.'

She looked down at the floor for several seconds, before she glanced back up. 'Wow, you don't hold back when you really get going, do you?'

He dragged a hand through his hair. 'I had a call on my way back. My father had a better health day today than the doctors have seen in the last six months. I missed it, Jasmine. I missed it because I'm attending dinners and vetting potential brides just so my people's faith in me can be restored. You think I should go easy on you for that?'

She'd grown paler as he spoke, and tears filled her eyes by the time he finished.

Reyes felt like a toad for upsetting her. He cursed silently when her mouth trembled.

'I wasn't going to apologise again. I think saying sorry loses its power after the first dozen times. But once again, please know that I never wished for this to happen to you, Reyes. I was protecting those I love and misjudged the consequences. But what's happening with your father is good news. You weren't there to witness it but that doesn't take away from the fact that he's better.'

About to denounce her for her unwanted optimism, he paused in surprise when she leaned in close and kissed his cheek.

His breath punched out as her alluring scent engulfed him. Too soon, she stepped back and he fought down a keen sense of loss.

Rocking back on his heels, Reyes eyed her. 'Why did you do that?' He was shocked enough for his voice to emerge flat. At every turn this woman threw him for a loop.

'You looked like you needed it. You'll be back home soon enough and in control of things. And Santo Sierra will get better with you in charge. I'm certain of it.'

She secured the towel around her, grabbed another one and

proceeded to dry her hair. He found himself transfixed, unable to take his eyes off her.

When she sat cross-legged on the lounger, Reyes fought to avert his gaze from her bare thighs. Seeing another scar on her knee, he frowned. From what he knew about her, he was aware her childhood hadn't been a bed of roses. But the physical marks caused him to wonder exactly what had happened to her.

'Did this happen to you in juvie?' he asked tersely as he sat opposite her.

She followed his gaze and shook her head. 'No. It was yet another product of my misspent youth.'

His fist clenched. 'That's not an answer, Jasmine.'

Her throat moved in a small swallow. 'I was pinned between two gangs during a turf war on the council estate where I lived. This is the result of flying glass from a shattered window.'

He forced himself to release his hold on the glass before it broke in his fist. 'Shattered glass from…?'

'Bullets.'

Icy fury washed over him. 'Your mother let you live in such a dangerous place?' His voice sounded gruff and almost alien in his ears.

'We had nowhere else to go.' No self-pity, just a statement of fact. And yet he knew that the situation must have been gruelling. Why else would she have fought to never return to a place like that again?

Overwhelmed by the protective instinct that continued to build inside him, Reyes looked at her knee. He barely resisted the urge to run his hand over the jagged scar. Just as he fought to ask whether there were more signs of her traumatic childhood on her body.

It wasn't his business. She was a transient presence in his life. He wasn't even interested in punishing her for the theft of his treaty any more. Her life had been a difficult one. She'd made choices she wasn't proud of, but she'd made those choices out of loyalty, a need to survive.

As much as he wanted to damn her for the turmoil she'd

left behind, deep down he knew that, faced with the same choice, he would choose the same path. How many times had he shielded his own father from his mother's misdeeds? Lied to protect his father's feelings? Even knowing what his mother had been doing the day she died, he'd tried to keep the truth from his father for as long as possible.

Except Reyes didn't want to let Jasmine go…not just yet.

What he wanted was to assuage the alarming, visceral need to flatten her on the nearest surface and rediscover the heady pleasures of her body.

His eyes rose to her face.

Awareness throbbed between them. Then she glanced away to the view of Paris at night.

'I was about to order room service. Do you want some food?' Her voice was husky, warm and sexy in that way that reminded him of their encounter in the darkened bedroom on his yacht.

He forced his gaze from her sensual mouth, and nodded. '*Sí*. I'm starving. Make sure you order an extra-large bread basket.'

She picked up the phone to make the call to his chef. Reyes traced the seductive line of her neck, and resisted the urge to jump into the pool to cool down his out-of-control libido.

Reyes dismissed the second candidate after a mere twenty minutes.

'What was wrong with her?' Jasmine asked, despite the heady pool of relief building inside her. Taking pains not to examine the feeling too closely, she hurried after him as he strode away from the restaurant on the Champs-Élysées.

'Your notes said she had nothing to do with her father's media business. That turned out not to be true.' He rounded on her once they were in the car and driving away. 'In case I haven't made it quite clear, I detest the media. They made my and my sister's lives a living hell when we were growing up, thanks to their insatiable interest in my mother and her infidelities.' His mouth was pinched and the lines around it deep and pale.

'I didn't know that about your mother. I'm sorry.'

He inhaled deeply and loosened the blue-striped tie he'd worn with a pristine white shirt and a dark grey suit. A muscle twitched in his jaw as he exhaled. '*Gracias*. Perhaps I did you a disservice by not giving you enough time to prepare for this.'

It was the closest he'd come to an apology for the unreasonable demands he'd made for her assignment. But even though she nodded her acceptance, Jasmine couldn't shift from his statement about his mother.

'Did your subjects know...about your mother?' she asked.

He wrenched at his top buttons and pulled his tie free. 'Yes, they knew. They thought my father weak for not divorcing her and by the time she died in her lover's car, she was very much a hated figure.'

'So by definition...'

'*Sí*, the whole House of Navarre hasn't endeared itself to the people.'

The question she'd been trying to avoid asking ricocheted through her head.

Ask. This is your chance.

'Back in Spain you said something about not wanting another destroyed life on your conscience. Did something else happen with your mother?'

His features froze and he remained silent for so long, she was certain he wouldn't answer.

'Five years ago, I almost got engaged.'

It was the last response she'd expected. Her mind blanked for a second. 'What?'

His laugh was bitter. 'You wanted to know why marrying wasn't my first choice, so...' He stopped and his face contorted with bitter recollection. Jasmine wanted to tell him to stop, wanted to wipe whatever wretched memory was causing the distress on his face. He spoke before she could form the appropriate words.

'Anaïs Perdot and I met the last time I was here in Paris. It was my first diplomatic tour. Her father was doing a lot of business in Santo Sierra and Anaïs and I grew...close.'

Jasmine didn't want to guess what memory was making his jaw clench. She held her breath as he continued. 'Her parents were eager for a match. I suppose on paper we were an ideal couple. She was young and exciting. For a while she made me forget that I was the son of a queen who didn't feel any remorse about dragging the family name through the mud with her infidelities. Hell, she even helped me to forge an easier relationship with the father I detested because I thought him weak for not stopping my mother's behaviour.' His chest heaved on a deep exhale.

'For a while?' she ventured.

His lips firmed. 'Her parents thought Anaïs should live in Santo Sierra for a while before we announced our engagement. Within weeks, my mother got her claws into her.'

'How?'

He shrugged. 'It started off as lunches and shopping sprees while I was busy with matters of state. Then they turned into late-night parties when she wouldn't return to the palace until the early hours, and then not at all.'

Jasmine frowned. 'Behaviour not exactly befitting a future queen, but European royalty have been known to indulge in much worse antics.'

His eyes turned arctic. 'Really? How many female members of your royal family have been photographed having sex with another man the week before their engagement was announced?'

Her hand flew to her mouth. 'Oh, my God! What did you do?'

Reyes stared at her for several more seconds before he shook his head. 'I handed over an obscene amount of money to the camera-wielding blackmailer to prevent the pictures hitting the papers. And I set back my relationship with my father by having our biggest fight yet when he refused to lift a finger against my mother for her part in Anaïs's behaviour.'

'I'm so sorry, Reyes.' She laid a hand on his arm and felt his palpable tension.

'That wasn't the worst of it. The day I told Anaïs it was over, she went to my mother. My mother convinced her that I was merely throwing a tantrum; that I would get over it. And then she talked Anaïs into partying one more night. On their way back from the club, they were involved in a hit-and-run accident. Anaïs claimed my mother was driving. My mother claimed the opposite. The result was that a teenager was left paralysed for life, his plans to become a doctor shattered.'

'And still your father did nothing?'

Reyes pinched the bridge of his nose. 'After I threw Anaïs and her family out of my life, she decided to share her version of her time in Santo Sierra with the media. My father finally tried to do some damage control, but it was too late. We were vilified in the media. My mother's behaviour spiralled out of control. A few months later, she was dead. That's when the first ramblings of unrest began.'

'And your father's illness just compounded the problems.'

That sadness she'd glimpsed on his face that first night in Rio appeared again. 'I never really got a chance to tell him that I regretted our fight. Last night would've been a good opportunity, had I been home.'

'You'll be home in a matter of days. You'll get your chance.'

He fell silent for a stretch of time, then he sent her an intense glance. The imperious ruler of one of the world's richest kingdoms was back. And despite the determined look on his face now, Jasmine couldn't help but feel desperate heartache for what he'd suffered. She realised her hand was still on his arm and lowered it to her lap.

'You understand now why finding the right candidate is imperative?' he asked.

Despite her heart taking a cliff-dive, she nodded. 'Yes, I do.'

Again her heart wrenched at the thought that weeks from

now he would be a married man. It would be a marriage of convenience, of course, but one he intended to commit to for a lifetime.

He would be out of reach for ever.

Last night, sharing a relaxing dinner with him, she'd wondered what it would've been like if they'd met under different circumstances. Then she'd kicked herself for the absurd thought.

Their backgrounds were too diverse for that to have happened in any lifetime. As she'd thought in Rio, they were two ships passing in the night, never to meet again.

But they'd met once...and again. Right at this moment, they could share a lifetime connection.

Because of Reyes's tight schedule and his edict that she wasn't allowed anywhere on her own, she hadn't been able to get her hands on the pregnancy test yet.

Instead she'd ordered it online and was expecting it to be delivered to the hotel today.

Until it arrived and she was forced to confront whatever consequences it brought, she would concentrate on carrying on as normal. Reality would come soon enough. Certainly before Reyes left for Santo Sierra.

And if her suspicions were right and she really was pregnant...

Reyes's door opened, and the driver bowed. 'Your Highness.'

Her heart lurched as she watched him struggle to suppress painful memories behind a bland façade. Again, the need to comfort him grew until she gripped her handbag to stop herself reaching for him.

Jasmine prayed the last candidate would be what Reyes wanted, while studiously ignoring the spear of pain that lanced her heart.

CHAPTER THIRTEEN

'WELL, I THINK we've discussed everything that needs to be discussed. I hope I've proven that I can be trusted and that I will be discreet, especially in matters of media liaisons.' Berenice Holden smiled at Reyes.

'You're comfortable with this arrangement being permanent? Or at the very least a long-term proposition?' Reyes asked.

'Of course. I like to think I'm bringing a lot to the table, but I'm aware I have much more to gain by ensuring any union between us works.'

Jasmine tried to keep her composure as the cold-blooded negotiations flew between Reyes and Berenice. They'd been hammering out terms for the last hour. And Jasmine had felt her heart wither each time they'd reached a compatible agreement.

She watched Reyes cross off the last item on his list, set his pen down and reach for his cutlery.

'Excuse me.' She rose and stumbled from the table. From the corner of her eye, she saw Reyes jerk to his feet, but she didn't stop until she slammed and locked the toilet door behind her. Shaking, she collapsed onto the closed lid.

Breathe...

This would be over soon. The test kits had arrived. Her attempt to take the test had been thwarted when Reyes had summoned her to grill her about Berenice before his meeting with her, and then insisted Jasmine accompany him.

Breathe...

In just over an hour she would know. Among other things, she didn't think it was healthy, if she was pregnant, to reside in this perpetual state of anxiety.

Her fingers trembled as the thought took root. She... pregnant...with Reyes's baby.

She closed her eyes and forced herself to breathe through her anxiety. Waiting until it was impolite to linger any longer, she returned to the table, sat through the last course. Tried to stop herself from trembling each time Berenice looked at Reyes.

Vaguely she noticed Reyes stand. 'Jasmine?'

She raised her head, met his probing glance. 'Yes?'

'Are you okay?' he asked.

Her head hurt when she nodded. He touched her arm to get her attention. All of a sudden, each of her senses zinged to life.

She looked round. Berenice had left. Jasmine was alone with Reyes again.

'Are you ready to leave? Or would you like dessert since you hardly touched your food?' He frowned down at her plate.

'I'm fine. I wasn't that hungry.' She rose and followed him out to the waiting limo. Heart in her throat, she slid in beside him. Silence throbbed in the car for several minutes, until she couldn't take it any more.

'So, you think she's the one?' Jasmine realised she'd stopped breathing as she waited for him to answer.

After a few moments, he shrugged. '*Sí*, she ticks all the boxes. I'll call a meeting of the council when we get back to Santo Sierra tomorrow. Tell them to start planning my wedding.'

She was pregnant.

Three sticks had confirmed it. Several online translations of the word *enceinte* along with three thick blue lines had sealed her fate.

Setting the tablet down on the bedcovers, Jasmine lay back on the bed and spread shaky fingers over her stomach.

Several emotions eddied through her, but gradually the fear, the anxiety, the complete and utter paralyzing notion that she was in no way equipped to be a mother, fell away to be replaced by one paramount sensation.

Joy.

She had a child growing inside her. Not just any child. Reyes's baby. The situation was completely messed up, but if fate had requested in a normal world that she choose the father of her child, Reyes Navarre would've been her first, her only choice.

Reyes…

She closed her eyes and inhaled deeply. She had to tell him. No question about that. The pain of never having known her father was one she'd smothered away during her childhood and teenage years. And although Stephen had filled the desolate hole left by her father's rejection, the dull ache remained.

She would never dream of subjecting her child to the same fate by choice. But then this wasn't just any child…

The enormity of what this pregnancy entailed burned through her joy.

God, she was pregnant with the future heir of the Santo Sierran throne. And its father was getting married to someone else in a matter of weeks.

Jasmine rolled to her side and hugged a pillow to her chest. Her eyes stung. She blinked rapidly. When her vision continued to blur, she dashed her fingers across her eyes, cursing the hormones running riot through her veins.

Think! She'd faced the worst dilemmas, protected herself and her mother from the most vicious thugs. She'd even faced bullies in juvie and emerged victorious. Stronger for it.

But did she possess the right skills to be a mother to a future king or queen? She squeezed her eyes shut and tried to ignore the tears. She wasn't a crier. Never had been…

She just needed a minute to absorb the life-changing news before—

'Jasmine!'

She started and opened her eyes to see Reyes crossing the vast suite towards her bed.

Sitting up, she eyed the tablet, breathing a sigh of relief to notice it'd gone dark. The actual pregnancy tests were safely tucked beneath her pillow.

'Have you heard of knocking?' she demanded. Her heart slammed into her ribs with its usual state of excitement at the sight of Reyes. But this time there was an added urgency. He was the father of her child. Which meant, one way or the other, they would be connected to each other for ever.

'I knocked. Several times. I entered because I was concerned. Are you okay?' He frowned down at her, those hawkish grey eyes tracking her face.

Too late, Jasmine remembered she'd been crying and probably had dried marks on her face. She dashed her hand across her cheeks.

'I'm...fine. Just a little tired.'

His frown didn't dissipate. Mouth dry, she slid her legs to the side of the bed and stood up. 'Did you want something?'

'You were supposed to supply my press secretary with Miss Holden's details. He hasn't received them yet.' His eyes narrowed further. 'Are you sure you're okay? You look pale.' He started to move forward, one hand raised to touch her.

She jerked out of reach, propelled solely by self-preservation. Her emotions were on enough of a roller coaster for her to risk disturbing them further by letting Reyes touch her. She needed to formulate her thoughts rationally before she broke the news to him. And Reyes touching her had never triggered rational thinking.

She risked a glance at him. His jaw was tense and his hand suspended mid-air. A look of hurt passed over his face before it was quickly veiled. She sucked in another breath. 'I'm fine. Really. I'll send the details now.'

He nodded tersely. Expecting him to leave, she gasped when he stepped closer and cupped her cheeks. 'You've been crying. Tell me what's wrong.'

'Reyes—'

'Don't tell me it's nothing. *Something* is wrong with you.

You've been jumpy lately. The chef tells me you hardly touched your breakfast and I know you didn't eat more than two mouthfuls at lunch. If you insist you're not sick, then it must be something else. Are you worried about what will happen to you when we get to Santo Sierra?'

'Should I be?' Honestly, she'd been too preoccupied with whether she was carrying his child to worry about whether Reyes would throw the book at her once they arrived at his homeland.

'I don't condone what you did, but I understand the motives behind it.'

She searched his gaze, and only saw steady reassurance. 'You do?'

He nodded. 'You were boxed into a corner, trying to save what was precious to you. It felt wrong when I chose to pay the blackmailers for those compromising photos of Anaïs instead of turning the whole thing over to the police but—'

'You were trying to protect your father from the pain of finding out.'

'*Sí*. And also myself to some extent.' His thumbs brushed her cheeks, traced the corner of her mouth. She locked her knees to keep them from giving way. 'You did what you had to do to protect your family. I can't condemn you for that.'

She swallowed hard as a lump rose in her throat. 'Thank you.'

His gaze drifted from her eyes to her mouth. In that moment, Jasmine didn't think she'd craved anything as she craved a kiss from him.

Her gaze caressed his mouth, and every nerve in her body screeched with delight. Then reality crashed. She couldn't kiss him. Would never be able to touch him again. He was marrying someone else.

Resolutely, she stepped back. 'I need to send the email. So if there's nothing else...?'

He tensed. Then, without a word, he left her room.

Jasmine collapsed on the bed, her hands fisted at her sides.

Ten minutes passed as she stared into space. Reyes had for-given her for what she did in Rio. Which meant, she could leave once she'd finalised the task he'd set her. And once she'd told him about the baby.

She had to leave. The longer she stayed around him, the more she yearned for things she had no business yearning for. As for the baby, parents hashed out living arrangements every day. She was sure they could come up with an arrangement that suited them both.

So why the hell were her eyes brimming again at the thought of returning to London on her own?

Shaking her head, she forced her thoughts aside and dealt with the email to Reyes's royal press secretary. Once it was done, she went to the bathroom, washed her face and brushed her hair. Taking a little bit of pride in her appearance bolstered her confidence. And for what she was about to do, she needed all the armour she could muster.

Her knock on his suite next door received a deep-voiced response to enter. She'd never seen the inside of Reyes's suite and stopped a few steps after entering.

Decorated in bold swathes of black and white, the luxuri-ous space was dominated by a king-sized bed with four solid posts made of cast iron.

The carpet was stark white and contrasted stunningly with the black velvet curtains. The design was bold, masculine and oozed quiet sophistication.

'Did you come to admire the décor?' Reyes said from where he stood at the window, gazing at the Parisian skyline.

Once her eyes fell on him, she couldn't look away. Dear God, she was like a crazed moth, obsessed with this particu-lar flame. A flame that didn't belong to her.

She cleared her throat. 'There's something I…need to tell you.' Her voice was little above a whisper.

He tensed. Then slowly turned and strode to where she'd stopped in the room. His hands remained in his pockets as his gaze raked her from head to toe. 'So speak.' His tone was rough, terse.

'I don't know how else to say this so I'm just going to spill it,' she said.

He stared at her. Silence stretched. He quirked an eyebrow.

Heart hammering, Jasmine closed her eyes for a split second and gathered her courage. 'I…we…'

'Jasmine?' he snapped.

'Yes?'

'Take a breath and find the words.'

'I'm pregnant.'

He was a crown prince. He was allowed a gamut of emotions. Courage under fire. Pride. Anger. Even bewilderment at times.

But Reyes was certain that somewhere in his kingdom's constitution, there was a clause that said he couldn't feel blind panic.

And yet that was the emotion that clawed through him once he convinced himself he hadn't misheard her. Panic and intense, debilitating jealousy.

Stop, he admonished himself. *Think for a moment.*

But he couldn't think beyond the naked fact that she'd slept with someone else, was pregnant with another man's child. That in the very near future she would no longer be in his life. She would belong to someone else.

He turned abruptly and headed for the living room adjoining his bedroom. 'Come with me.'

She followed. When they reached the set of sofas, he jerked his chin at the nearest one.

'Sit down.'

'I don't need to—'

'Sit down, Jasmine. Please.'

She sat, crossed her ankles, and folded her hands in her lap. He tried not to stare at the silky fall of her hair. The perfection of her face.

She belonged to someone else.

A piercing pain lanced his chest. He paced to the window, as if the different view would provide cold perspective.

'Obviously this changes things. You wish me to release you from your obligations?' The words felt thick and unnatural. Not at all what he wanted to be asking her.

When she remained silent, he turned. Her mouth was parted in surprise. And shock?

'Umm, eventually, yes. But I'm not doing anything that would risk the baby's health, so I can see this task through.' She stopped and bit her lip. 'If you want me to, that is.'

Did he want a woman he'd made love to, who was now carrying another man's child, completing her task of seeing him wed another woman?

Dios. When had his life turned into a three-ring circus?

'Who is he?' he bit out before the words had fully formed in his mind.

Realising the panic had been totally annihilated by jealousy didn't please him. Nor did he welcome her confusion.

'Who is who?'

'The father of your baby.' Why did the words burn his throat so badly?

Her eyes widened. 'The father? You mean you think…' She shook her head. 'It's you, Reyes. You're the father of my baby.'

He willed the cymbals crashing through his head to stop. *'What did you say?'*

'I said this baby is yours. Ours.'

Panic. Bewilderment. Panic. Pride.

Elation. Pride. Anger.

'Mine. Do you take me for a fool?' he rasped.

'No, of course not. Reyes—'

'Or did you think you'd wait until I'd forgiven you before you sprang this *happy surprise* on me?'

'I really don't know what you're talking about,' she replied. Her bafflement was almost convincing.

'You know exactly what I'm talking about. Was that the

plan all along? To innocently run into me at the embassy in London and plot your way to a higher payday?'

She shook her head. 'Plans and plots? Next you'll be accusing me of mind-controlling you into forgetting to use a condom in the shower back in Rio.'

The bolt of shock rocked him backwards. Frantically, he searched his memory.

The shower...no condom...Madre di Dios...

He stared at her, rooting for the truth. 'The child is mine?' he croaked.

Her eyes met his. Bold and fierce. 'Yes. I know my credibility isn't worth much to you, but believe me when I say that I'd never stoop to such deplorable deception. No matter what.'

He nodded, still reeling. He believed her. But the inherent need to seek the absolute truth pounded through him. The past still had a stranglehold on him he couldn't easily let go of. 'You weren't on the pill?'

'No. I didn't need to be.'

He paced in a tight circle. 'When did you find out?' he asked.

'I did the tests an hour ago.'

She pulled three pink-and-white sticks from her jeans pocket and held them up.

Reyes forced himself to move. He took them, examined them. And slid them into his own pocket.

Somehow their presence finally hammered reality home.

He was going to be a father.

Jasmine wasn't carrying another man's child. She was carrying *his*.

Elation. A strange, undeniable possessiveness.

'I'll arrange for the doctor to see you. We need to address that poor appetite of yours.'

Jasmine licked her lips. 'There's no hurry. It can wait—'

'No, it cannot wait. Nothing can wait. Not any more.'

'What does that mean?' she enquired.

'It means everything has changed.' Reaching down, he

stroked her cheek. He wasn't sure why it hadn't occurred to him before. Jasmine wasn't the perfect candidate but she was miles better than anyone he knew. There would be no false proclamations of love to confuse issues. They were compatible in bed.

And she was carrying his child…

Her silky skin made his pulse jump. Or was it his own senses jumping from the situation presented so perfectly before him? So perfect, he wanted to kiss her!

Walking away before he was tempted to give in to the hunger churning through him, Reyes strode to the polished teak desk.

'Reyes, you're not making much sense.'

They both stopped at the knock on the door. 'Yes?'

His young aide entered. 'The council is here. I've put them in the conference room, as you requested.'

Reyes nodded. '*Gracias*, Antonio. I'll be there shortly.'

Antonio retreated and Reyes rounded the desk. There was so much he wanted to say, and yet he couldn't find the right words to say it. In the end, he crouched in front of Jasmine and took both her hands in his.

'This was as much my responsibility as yours. I failed in my duty to protect you, and for that I apologise. I got carried away…but I can assure you I don't have any adverse health issues you should worry about.'

'Neither have I,' she blurted.

He nodded. 'Good. I hope you're agreeable to what needs to happen next, too.'

She frowned. 'I'm not sure I follow.'

'It means I'm calling off next week's wedding. And I'm getting married in three days instead.'

Jasmine felt the blood drain from her head. It was a good thing he was holding on to her because she was sure she would've collapsed in an agonising, pathetic heap.

'I… Okay. Leave it with me. I'll call Miss Holden and arrange for her to fly to Santo Sierra,' she replied through numb lips. Her whole body was going numb and she really needed to sit down before she fell.

Reyes's brows bunched. 'Why would you be calling her?'

'Because you're marrying her?'

'You misunderstand, Jasmine. The wedding is for you. *I intend to marry no one else but you.*'

As proposals went, it wasn't the most romantic she'd heard. But even through the shock engulfing her, she realised there would be nothing resembling romance, or love, in whatever Reyes planned for them.

CHAPTER FOURTEEN

THE PICTURES JASMINE had seen of Santo Sierra didn't do it justice even in the slightest.

As the royal jet circled majestic green mountains and turquoise waters in preparation for landing, she could barely contain her awe.

'Now I get a reaction from you. I thought I'd have to surgically remove you from that tablet.'

She turned sharply from her avid landscape gazing. 'I'm sorry?'

'You've hardly spoken a word since we took off.' He frowned. 'In fact, you seem to have lost the ability to speak the last twenty-four hours.' His gaze raked her face. 'Are you feeling unwell?'

She struggled to keep her features composed and not show how much turmoil she'd been in since he'd announced *she* was his choice of bride.

Her bewildered 'Why?' had been met with incredulity.

'Are you serious?'

'Of course, I'm serious. You have your perfect candidate already picked out.'

'And you are carrying my baby. My heir.' His brows had clamped together. *'What did you think was going to happen when you told me?'* he'd asked with a heavy dose of astonishment.

And there their discussion had ended.

The council had been waiting. He'd summoned Antonio to call the doctor, who'd arrived just as the council meeting had ended.

Reyes had peppered him with questions and he'd listened with an intensity that had terrified Jasmine. Even before the poor doctor had been dismissed, she'd known Reyes was heavily vested in his baby's welfare. And that she wouldn't be returning to London to raise her child as a single parent.

She was going to Santo Sierra to marry Prince Reyes Navarre.

She, a juvenile delinquent with a chequered past, was going to be crowned Princess in just over forty-eight hours.

And if that weren't terrifying enough, the realisation of what she was trying desperately to deny had finally hit her in the face this morning. She was developing potentially heart-risking feelings for Reyes. Ironically, her mother had called this morning just as she was busy denying her feelings.

Jasmine would never have thought in a million years that she would adopt her mother's head-in-the-sand approach to life one day.

'Jasmine?'

God, the Latin intonation to the way he said her name...

'No, I'm just a little nervous.'

He waved her nerves away. 'Don't be. The palace staff will cater to your every need. And my sister, Isabella, will also be on hand should you need a female perspective on any concerns.' He smiled.

Her breath caught.

Scared he'd read any unwanted emotion on her face, she looked out of the window again, towards the mountain she'd learned was called Montana Navarre. Set on the highest peak, it was where the Royal House of Navarre had been born and where Reyes's ancestors had ruled Santo Sierra for several centuries. Airplanes were restricted from flying directly over the palace, but the aerial view she'd seen of it had taken her breath away.

With supreme effort, she looked at him. 'Are you sure we're not rushing this? I'm sure there must be special protocols to royal weddings that I need to learn first?'

His eyelids descended and his nostrils flared slightly before he pierced her with that incisive grey gaze once more. 'You're carrying my child, Jasmine. Everything else ceases to matter in light of that reality.'

She couldn't read anything into that thick emotion in his voice. It was just shock.

Recalling how his councilmen had beamed at her when they'd emerged from their meeting, Jasmine added another reason as to why Reyes was pleased about the turn of events.

Next to a royal wedding, a royal baby was the most joyous celebration for any country. Reyes was returning home not just with his future bride, but with his future heir, although the formal announcement of her pregnancy wouldn't be made for another few weeks.

Coupled with his economic plans for Santo Sierra, those two events would surely regain him his people's love and devotion.

A part of her felt relieved and thankful that her actions wouldn't leave permanent damage on Santo Sierra. The other, selfish part of her couldn't hide the pain of feeling like collateral damage.

'You're still troubled,' Reyes observed.

She'd forgotten how well he could read her. Clearing her throat, she passed restless fingers through her hair. 'It's my problem. I'll deal with it.'

His face darkened. 'You're no longer an individual, fighting against the masses on your own. And I prefer not to start our marriage with secrets between us.'

She shook her head. 'Trust me, Reyes, you don't really want to know what's going on in my head right now. I'm hormonal and perhaps conveniently irrational.'

Firm, sensual lips pursed. 'I want to hear it, Jasmine.'

The voice of caution probed, and was promptly ignored. 'Fine, if you insist. I was right in front of you, Reyes. And yet you never considered me as a bride. So excuse me if I'm feeling a pauper's sloppy seconds.'

* * *

Oh, God. Why on earth did I say that?

Jasmine was still reeling hours after they'd landed and she'd been delivered to her suite in the palace.

Despite her opulent surroundings and the rich history etched into every arched wall, mosaic-tiled floor, and ancestral painting, she couldn't see, couldn't think beyond the stark, soul-baring words she'd uttered moments before the plane had touched down.

How utterly pathetic she'd sounded.

The shock on Reyes's face alone had convinced her she'd stepped way over the line. No wonder he'd beat a hasty retreat the moment they'd reached the palace.

She rose from the beautifully carved brocade love seat by the window in her vast bedroom and entered the bathroom.

The marble-lined tub had already been filled with scented water and huge fluffy towels laid within arm's length by the palace staff assigned to cater to her needs.

She'd been lost for words when she'd walked into a closet filled with designer clothes and accessories. And even more stunned when the member of staff had told her they'd been provided for her.

Shrugging off the silk robe, she sank into the enveloping warmth. She'd been summoned to dine with Reyes and his sister this evening, no doubt to be checked out by her future sister-in-law.

Jasmine looked out of the wide tub-to-ceiling trellised bathroom window and her breath caught all over again. With nothing to mar the mountaintop view she could see the kingdom for miles.

The bustling, vibrant capital of San Domenica was spread below her. Whitewashed churches vied with modern architecture, green parks and historical buildings.

As they'd driven through it on the way to the palace she'd glimpsed the look of pride and worry in Reyes's eyes. They'd also driven past the square and his fingers had tightened on the armrest when he'd seen a woman crying next to a broken statue.

Her insides had clenched for him. But he'd relaxed against the seat, his face averted from her as they'd climbed up the highway leading to the palace.

The moment they'd been escorted inside, he'd made his excuses and strode off.

And she'd been left grappling with her mangled feelings. Feelings she still hadn't been able to resolve by the time she dressed in a long sweeping gown in emerald green with a coloured-stone-embroidered bodice that had made her gasp when she'd spied herself in the mirror.

Sweeping her hair up into a bun, she secured it with several hairpins and slipped her feet into black slingbacks.

Fernanda, the staff member appointed to shepherd her to the dining room, left her with a smile and walked away after delivering Jasmine to the high-ceilinged room displaying ancient Mediterranean frescos.

Jasmine was busy admiring it when she heard voices outside the dining room.

Going to the door, she followed the sound down a long hallway, hurrying closer to where the raised voices came from. Rounding the corner, she came upon Reyes and a tall, slim woman in the middle of a heated argument.

He wore a thunderous look as he glared down at the stunning woman. A stunning woman who was giving as good as she got, her voice rising higher as she gestured wildly and responded in Spanish.

Jasmine thought of retreating. But they both turned as they sensed her presence.

For a moment, Reyes appeared frozen at the sight of her. His hooded eyes raked her from head to toe. Then he exhaled, his massive chest drawing her eyes to his impressively broad shoulders. His black shirt moulded his lean torso and washboard stomach before disappearing into dark grey tailored trousers that caressed his powerful thighs. His hair looked damp from a recent shower. He slicked it back now as he spiked his fingers through it.

Jasmine forced herself not to remember how those strands felt beneath her fingers.

'Hi,' she ventured. The breathlessness in her voice made her cringe.

Reyes's mouth compressed before he turned to the woman. 'Isabella, meet Jasmine Nichols, my future wife. Jasmine, this is my sister, Princess Isabella. She'll escort you to the terrace for drinks. I'll join you shortly.' Without waiting for a response, he stalked off down the opposite end of the hallway.

Isabella watched him leave, her expression hurt and angry. She looked spectacular in a cream gown laced with gold and black thread. The satin material fitted her svelte figure and complemented her golden, flawless skin.

Turning to Jasmine, she shook her head in frustration. 'Apparently, I was wrong to call off a wedding to a man I did not love.'

Jasmine's insides clenched. 'Duty is very important to your brother.' She tried a diplomatic approach.

Isabella threw up her hands in despair. 'Well, duty doesn't keep you warm. From the examples we've both had, you'd think he'd know that marriage is hard enough without going into it with a cold heart. I told him if I had to wait a thousand years for a man who makes me happy, I would.'

A spurt of laughter erupted from Jasmine's throat. 'Bet he didn't take that lightly.'

Isabella smiled. 'As you saw, storming off was his reaction.' She released an exasperated breath, then eyed Jasmine. 'Or maybe it was something else?' One perfectly shaped eyebrow rose.

'I'm not sure what you mean,' Jasmine replied.

'You'll find out soon enough how difficult it is to keep a secret in this place. You are not the woman my brother's press office was gearing up to announce as his bride two days ago.

Which makes me wonder if whatever's irking him has nothing to do with me and everything to do with you?'

Jasmine licked her lips, uncomfortable about having this conversation with Isabella when she was unsure what her role entailed in this marriage of convenience. She'd have to pick it up with Reyes. Once he could have a conversation with her again without that look of consternation.

'Please, can we drop the subject?'

The other woman wrapped her hand around Jasmine's arm. 'Of course, I didn't mean to upset you. *Dios*, I can't seem to breathe for causing upset today.'

'No, please. Think nothing of it.' She flashed a smile.

Isabella's shrewd gaze rested on her for a moment before she nodded. 'Fine. Come, we'll enjoy some cocktails before dinner. If Reyes gets over his tantrum, he can join us. Otherwise it's his loss.'

Jasmine followed her down the hallway to a large, skylit room with wide doors that led onto a wide terrace. Soft lights glinted through the space dotted with large, potted ficus trees. In the centre an extensive bar had been built, manned by two servants.

One came forward with a tray holding an array of gaily coloured drinks. Isabella pointed to the iced green one.

'Try that one. It's made with guava and a local fruit called *santosanda*.'

'It's not alcoholic, is it?' Seeing the instant speculation in Isabella's eyes, she hurriedly added, 'I'll never get over the jet lag if I add alcohol to the mix.'

Isabella shook her head. 'It doesn't contain any alcohol.'

Jasmine picked up the drink and took a sip. Different textures exploded on her tongue, the dominant one a tangy sweetness that sent a delicious chill down her spine. 'Wow.'

Isabella smiled and sipped her own peach-tinged drink. She drifted out onto the terrace, and she stood staring at the horizon.

Lights came on as darkness fell and her thoughtful gaze

rested over the view of San Domenica. 'In case you're wondering, I'm really pleased about your wedding to my brother. The council is right. We need a boost of good news. We've lived with doom and gloom since Mamá died.' She shook her head. 'I know I followed my heart in not marrying Alessandro, but I had been wondering lately if I took the selfish route.'

Jasmine shook her head. 'You would've caused each other too much pain in the end. Once the rose shades come off, relationships are an uphill struggle of hard work.' *Especially without love.*

'Are you speaking from experience?'

Despite her subtle probing, Jasmine warmed to Isabella. The princess had an open, honest face that went with her take-no-prisoners attitude.

'I watched my mother turn herself inside out for men who didn't deserve her love.'

Isabella's mouth pursed. 'My mother had all the love a man could give a woman, yet she went searching for more. Over and over, and in the wrong places. My father has never overcome the knowledge that he wasn't enough for her.'

'One-sided love is just as hard to keep up as no love at all.' Her heart lurched as she said the words, but Jasmine refused to examine why too deeply. She was too scared to find out. She went to take another sip and realised she'd finished the cocktail. The servant stepped forward with another. She smiled her thanks, took it, and turned back to the view.

'How is your father?'

Isabella looked towards the south wing of the palace, and sadness cloaked her face. 'He's hanging in there. I don't mean to sound callous and it'll break my heart when it happens, but I just wish he'd let go. I want him to find peace—'

'Isabella!'

She jumped at the admonishing voice.

Reyes stood behind them, his face more thunderous than it had been before.

'I'm...sorry, *mi hermano*, but you know I'm right.'

Reyes's fists bunched. 'If those are the sorts of views you choose to share with Jasmine, then perhaps you should consider eating dinner on your own.'

Eyes widening, Isabella gulped. Then her face closed with rebellion. 'Fine. I think I will.'

Before Jasmine could draw breath, the princess had stormed off.

Her gaze collided with Reyes's. 'Upsetting women seems to be your speciality. Are you sure you don't want to relocate to a faraway monastery and live the rest of your life as a monk?'

His expression lightened a touch. Grey eyes surveyed her from top to toe before they lingered at the drink in her hand. 'The silence I can probably handle. The chastity would unfortunately be a deal-breaker. How many of those have you had?' He nodded to her drink.

'This is my second one. Isabella recommended it. That local fruit…*santosanda*? It's delicious.'

'It is, but did she mention that, once fermented, it's also a powerful aphrodisiac?' he asked silkily.

CHAPTER FIFTEEN

REYES WATCHED HER eyes widen in shock, before a flush of awareness reddened her cheeks. She glanced at the drink, then back to him.

'No, she didn't!' Her voice had grown huskier. She blinked slowly as she passed her tongue over her plump lower lip.

Dios, had she even noticed the effects taking hold of her?

She'd been languidly caressing the lip of her glass for the last several minutes. And her nipples were hard and clearly outlined beneath her dress.

Reyes swallowed. 'I think you've had enough,' he rasped. He took the half-empty glass and handed it to the hovering waiter. Picking up two glasses of water, he thrust one into her hand.

'Umm…thanks.'

He nodded tersely.

Walking onto the terrace, he'd been hit between the eyes again by her stunning beauty. So much so, he'd stood frozen while her conversation with Isabella had unravelled.

It wasn't until his sister's utterance that he'd shaken off the red haze of lust that seemed to enclose him when he was around Jasmine.

Watching her now, he recalled what she'd said to him before they'd landed in Santo Sierra.

And the resulting tailspin his emotions had been flung in. Once he'd been able to draw breath, he'd tried to analyse his reaction. Yes, the knowledge of Jasmine's pregnancy had been the catalyst that had driven everything forward. But he could just as easily have maintained the initial date of his wedding. He was a modern enough man to admit the distance between his wedding day and his heir's birthday didn't bother him. And he was sure it didn't bother Jasmine.

So why had he been intent on rushing her to the altar?

He'd tried and failed to convince himself it was because of his need to make his people happy. A week's difference wouldn't have mattered. Neither did it matter that Jasmine's past would be an issue once it became public knowledge. Unlike his mother's behaviour, Jasmine's reasons for her unfortunate past were a result of trying to survive her horrific circumstances. He was sure his people would forgive once they knew.

Just as he'd forgiven her? Just as he suspected his reasons for marrying were more selfish than he wanted to admit to himself?

Reyes thrust his balled fists into his pocket, willed the confusing emotions away, but they returned stronger. More demanding.

He didn't do feelings. Hadn't let any in, except maybe for his father, since he'd thrown Anaïs out of his life, and then stood at his mother's graveside mere months later.

But Jasmine was making him feel. Making him want... no, *need*. As for the thought that his child was growing in her belly...it pounded him with terrifyingly powerful emotions every time it blazed across his mind.

Would the mistakes that he'd made with his own father affect his child? Was failure emblazoned in his blood for ever?

More and more he'd found himself wanting to take Jasmine's example. She had found a way out of the barren wasteland of not having anyone to lean on, anyone to trust. But she'd let herself trust, allowed her faith in the goodness of humanity to be restored. Despite the harrowing experience of juvenile detention and a mother who clearly wasn't equipped for the job, she'd found herself back on a road Reyes himself was struggling to find.

He couldn't deny it. She compelled him to be a better

man. Would raising their child together make him a better father, too?

Swallowing his blind panic, he glanced at her.

Her eyes were on him, her fingers curled around the glass. 'I feel funny.'

Unaccustomed laughter rumbled out of his chest. 'You need fresh air. Dinner won't be for another hour. Come, I'll show you the grounds.'

She peered down at her feet. 'I don't think these shoes will go well with walking the grounds. They're already pinching something fierce.'

'You won't need to walk further than the bottom of these steps.' Golf buggies were housed at various points around the palace for ease of movement around the extensive grounds.

He guided her down and waited till she was seated on the buggy. Reyes wasn't at all surprised when she kicked off her shoes and sighed with relief.

The sight of her dainty feet gripped his attention. Mesmerised, he watched her rub her big toe along her other instep. Heat flared through his gut and pooled in his groin. Pulling himself out of the daze, he reversed the buggy and stepped on the accelerator.

Floodlights illuminated their path as he drove towards the northernmost point of the palace. Beside him, Jasmine oohed and aahed at the elaborate fountain his great-grandfather had built for his children to splash in, the huge lake containing white majestic swans gliding serenely in the rising moonlight, and ruins of an amphitheatre set into a cliff.

Jasmine pointed to the spotlights strung along the outer edge of the theatre. 'Do you still use it?'

He nodded. 'Isabella holds a children's Christmas concert every year.'

'That's so cool. Everything about Santo Sierra is so cool,' she amended with a husky chuckle. Then she glanced at him. 'But snapping at Isabella like that? Not cool.'

Reyes's fingers tightened around the wheel, but his reaction was more to do with her laugh and less to do with his sister.

He brought the buggy to a stop on the grassy landscape and helped her out. She started to put on her shoes.

'Leave them. You won't need them where we're going.'

With a happy smile, she dropped them.

Hiking up her dress to keep the hem off the grass, she stepped out.

Reyes tried not to stare at her feet. 'We have a temperamental relationship, Bella and I. She'll have calmed down by now.'

Jasmine frowned. 'But you won't apologise? I think you should.'

'*Sí*, I will apologise. In the morning, when I'm convinced she won't bite my head off.'

She laughed.

He stopped in his tracks as the intoxicating sound transfixed him.

When she realised he'd stopped moving, she froze. 'What?'

He cleared his throat to dislodge the uncomfortable knot. 'You should laugh more. It's an entrancing sound.'

She blushed as her eyes rounded, then her expression turned gloomy. 'I haven't had much to laugh about. Not since...' She stopped and bit her lip.

He held his breath. 'Since?'

'Since Rio,' she muttered. 'And especially since I found out what my actions caused.'

The sincerity in her voice shook the foundation of his armour. He searched her face. Her eyes met his with frank appraisal and in that moment he was sure she'd never been more sincere.

He held out his hand, his breath lodged in his chest.

She hesitated, and his hand wavered. Looking down, she indicated her dress. 'I don't want to let go in case I get grass stains on it.'

His breath punched out. 'It's just a dress, Jasmine. I'll buy you a hundred more. Let go.'

She made a face. 'Yes, Your Bossiness.' She released her grip on the dress and slid her hand into his. Warm. Firm. Almost trusting...

A simple gesture. And yet he couldn't stop thinking about it as he walked her twenty yards up the small hill.

'Where are we going?' she asked breathlessly.

He realised he'd been marching and slowed his pace. 'Up there.' He pointed.

She stopped and gazed at the stone monument planted in the earth. 'What is it?'

'You need to get closer to see it.'

She followed him. When she tried to free their linked fingers, he held on, unwilling to let her go. Smiling at him over her shoulder, she stepped closer to the stone and ran her fingers over the ancient markings set into the rough surface.

Still clinging to her fingers, Reyes walked her round the stone, then led her to the jagged crevice.

'Oh, my God,' she whispered. Reyes watched the wonder on her face as she peered into the black three-foot-wide crack scorched into the earth. 'How deep is it?'

Stepping behind, he let go of her hand and wrapped his arms around her waist. 'No one knows. All past rulers of Santo Sierra have forbidden the site from being explored.'

She leaned back in his arms and stared up at him. 'But how did it get here?'

He bent his head, and his lips brushed the top of her ear. 'Legend has it that the original Crown Prince of Santo Sierra ran off with the betrothed of the Prince of Valderra the day before they were to be married. The jilted prince hunted them down and caught up with the lovers at this spot. They fought to the death and both lost their lives. The day after they were buried, the subjects woke up to find the fissure here. The two kingdoms have been separated ever since.'

Her arms folded over his and she rested her head on his shoulder. She rocked slowly from side to side in a silent dance.

'That's tragic, but I bet it can all be resolved with a good mediation.'

He laughed, found himself moving along with her, swaying to her inner music. 'You believe you can succeed where countless others have failed?'

'Mediation is about breaking things down to the basest level and routing out what each party needs the most. Once it's clear, most people will settle for their innermost desires instead of what their greed dictates they need.' Her voice had softened to an introspective murmur.

Reyes stared down at her sweet face, her perfect nose and gorgeous mouth. Something moved within him. Not his libido, even though it was awake and alert to any imminent action.

His innermost desire included kissing her, making her his. Permanently...

He realised she was growing drowsy from the drink and visibly forced his gaze away from temptation. 'What are your innermost desires, Jasmine?' he asked before he could stop himself.

'World peace. Or barring that a magical carriage to whisk me back down this hill so I don't have to walk.' She giggled, and a smile cracked across his face again.

Dios, he was in danger of slipping deeper into her web. Maybe this trip hadn't been such a good idea.

Or maybe he just needed to take a leaf out of his sister's book and follow his heart rather than his head for once. He and Jasmine might have arrived at this arrangement unconventionally, but fate had gifted them a compatibility that he would be foolish to ignore.

Tomorrow morning, there would be a vote to elect a new council, after which he'd be named Prince Regent. The palace press had already announced his impending wedding. His father's doctors had assured him that the King's health was holding for the moment and he'd seen a slight improvement in his father's condition when he'd visited him today.

As for Mendez, the Valderran prince knew something was

up. He'd been putting out feelers as to Santo Sierra's position on the old treaty. Reyes had ignored him so far. Let him stew for a while.

For now, Reyes intended to enjoy an evening free of guilt and anxiety. With the woman who would become his in less than forty-eight hours.

The woman who was carrying his child.

He paused as a bolt of satisfaction lanced through him. Reyes realised having Jasmine and their child in his life was a prospect that didn't terrify him as much as it had this time yesterday. Yesterday, he'd convinced himself it was duty driving him.

Today, his feelings were more of...elation.

Bending, he swung Jasmine into his arms. She gave another giggle and curled her arms around his neck. Her nose brushed his jaw and his belly tightened.

Si, a worry-free few hours were just what he needed.

'We don't have a carriage, but I have something in mind that might please you.' He strode to the top of the hill, turned ninety degrees and nudged her with his chin. 'There,' he murmured in her ear.

Jasmine pried her gaze from Reyes's breath-stoppingly gorgeous face and jawline and glanced where he'd indicated.

She was aware her mouth had dropped open. Again.

Could she help it when Santo Sierra had so far delivered one stunning surprise after another?

'It looks like a giant, gorgeous wedding cake,' she whispered.

'Because it was designed as a present for a bride's wedding day. But it's actually a summer house.'

'Set into the hillside so it looks like layers. It's perfect.'

The smile that had flashed on and off for the last half hour curved back into sight. Again her heart beat wildly, sending her blood roaring in her ears.

Although she was thankful he wasn't growling at her or

walking away from her as if she didn't exist, she was terrified at seeing this new, relaxed side of Reyes. This Reyes was too much for her senses. Too breathtaking. Too charming. Too... close.

But not too much that she wanted to get away. Or return to her lonely palace suite. She tightened her arms when he started towards the utterly splendid structure.

If she'd truly believed in fairy tales, this would've been her dream house. But she didn't, so it was just as well that the effects of the punch had worn off enough for her to realise this was nothing but a short interlude in time for both of them.

He climbed the stairs to the surprisingly large square structure and the wooden shuttered doors slid back. Jasmine's gaze slid from the love seat on the porch to the interior.

Bypassing the simple, lamplit living room furnished with more love seats and twin sofas festooned with cushions, Reyes walked her into the bathroom and set her down on a pedestal next to a wide porcelain sink.

He stepped back and turned on the tap in the extra-wide bath.

'Umm...is one of us taking a bath?'

His mouth tilted. 'I thought you might want to wash your feet since you've been walking in the grass.'

Jasmine looked down at her feet. 'Oh, I guess that's a good idea, what with the wall-to-wall white carpeting.'

She started to step down from her perch. He stayed her with a hand on her waist and leaned over to add bath salts to the warm water.

This close, his scent assailed her, claimed her senses. When he breathed his body moved against hers.

This was getting out of hand...

Despite the thought trailing through her head, she stayed where she was.

Once the water reached a quarter way, he turned to her. 'Lift up your dress.'

She tugged the material up her hips. He picked her up and

sat her on the edge of the tub. Expecting him to leave her to it, she gave a small gasp when he dropped to his knees beside her.

Grabbing a washcloth, Reyes dipped it in the scented water and started to clean her feet.

The punch of feeling through her chest made her jerk. He looked up, took her arm and slid it around his shoulders. 'Hold on to me if you think you're slipping.'

Nodding dumbly, she held on. Traced her fingers over the strands of hair at his nape. Her fingers brushed his skin. A rough sound escaped his throat. The soothing cloth cleansed her feet.

Jasmine looked from Reyes's arresting profile to what he was doing. She, Jasmine Nichols, originally from one of the roughest neighbourhoods in London, had a bona fide prince washing her feet.

The moment couldn't get more surreal than this. And yet she didn't want it to end.

'You have the most perfect feet,' Reyes murmured.

'Thank you.' Her voice emerged as shaky as she felt inside.

He raised his head and pierced her with eyes wild with raw, predatory hunger. 'The most perfect legs.' His wet hands cupped her ankles, drifted up over her calves.

Jasmine forgot to breathe. Her hand gripped his nape, her only stability in a world careening out of control.

'The most perfect thighs.'

'Reyes…'

His gaze dropped to her lips. Her heartbeat spiked a second before his mouth claimed hers.

Groaning, she fell into the kiss, wrapped both arms around his neck when he lifted her out of the tub and out of the bathroom. He returned to the living room and lowered her in front of the fireplace.

Lowering his body on top of hers, he deepened the kiss, ravaged her mouth with an appetite that grew sharper, rougher by the minute. His hand trailed up her leg, her thigh, to close over her bottom.

They both groaned when he squeezed her flesh. '*Dios*, you're perfect,' he breathed into the side of her neck when he let her up for air.

But she didn't want breathing room, didn't want even the slightest doubt to mar this incredible moment.

Catching his jaw between her hands, she raised her mouth to his. 'Kiss me, Reyes. Please.'

He swore again, the sound ragged. Scooping her against his chest, he rolled them over. Firm hands lowered her zip and tugged down her dress and flung it away. Then he reversed their position again. 'Now I can kiss you properly. Everywhere.'

He devoured her lips, her throat, the tops of her breasts.

Her moans grew louder as he rolled her nipple in his mouth before sucking in a hot pull. Jasmine's back arched, her fingers digging into his hair to keep him there, pleasuring her, torturing her. A sharp cry erupted from her lips when his teeth nipped her skin just above her panties. Rising up on her elbows, she stared down at him, drunk on the sight of what he was doing to her.

'Reyes…'

He glanced up. The look on his face threatened to send her over the edge.

'Do you want this, *querida*?' he enquired thickly.

'More than anything,' she whispered.

She smothered the voice that cautioned her as to what she was doing. Her first time with this man had ended in disaster. Granted, it'd been one of her own making. But now she knew it was more than her body involved. Her heart was at risk, too.

She was in danger of falling in love with a man who would never love her.

'I can hear you thinking.' He paused in the line of kisses he was dotting along her pantyline. 'Tell me what's on your mind.'

'I don't want anything we do here today to…confuse issues.'

His eyes narrowed. 'Shouldn't that be my line?'

Unwilling to help herself, she cupped his shadowed cheek.

'You may be a crown prince, but I believe in equal opportunities when it comes to the bedroom.'

He turned his head, kissed her palm and raised both her hands above her head. 'Well, this is my opportunity. You get your turn later.'

He took her mouth in a hard kiss, then raised his head. 'In answer to your question, there is no issue to confuse. We already know we're compatible in bed. Whether we say our vows tomorrow or the next day, we both want this, now. *Sì?*' His eyes probed hers.

Her heart lurched. 'Yes.'

CHAPTER SIXTEEN

REYES WATCHED HER expression turn from hesitant to erotically pleased as he cupped her breast and teased the hard nub.

The voice that told him he wasn't giving her room to change her mind was ruthlessly squashed. His hunger for her had flamed higher than every other need. And just as he'd taken her in Rio, he intended to let nothing stand in the way of his claiming her tonight.

He resumed his exploration of her body. Much to his very male satisfaction she arched her back and purred. And grew increasingly, pleasingly demanding.

She grabbed at his clothes and he hurriedly undressed. He yanked away her panties and positioned himself between her legs.

'Yes. Please…now,' she cried hoarsely.

Reyes surged inside her with a guttural roar. Sensation exploded all over his body at her wetness, her tight heat. She embraced him, rolled her hips in helpless abandon as pleasure overtook her.

He established a passionate rhythm she matched with enthusiasm. Much too soon, he was following her into bliss, shouting his ecstasy as he emptied himself inside her.

He watched her as they caught their breaths. Her face glowed with the flushed aftermath of sex. Reyes had never seen a more beautiful woman. His groin stirred. Her eyes slowly widened.

Smiling, he pressed a kiss against her heated cheek. 'You have that effect on me.' He pulled out of her. They both groaned at the sizzle of electricity.

Tucking her against his side, he caught her free hand in his, kissed her soft palm. Almost inevitably, his hand slid over her flat stomach. He heard her breath catch and searched her face.

A look of wonder, much like what he was experiencing at that very moment at the thought of his child growing inside her, passed over her face. For several heartbeats, he held her gaze. Then she blinked.

'Reyes?'

'*Si?*'

'I know you're a prince and all, but please tell me you're as terrified as I am at the thought of getting it wrong with this baby.'

'I will not discuss my silent mental breakdown with you, except to mention that it's very acute. And very unsexy.'

She laughed. The sound filled his chest with pleasure so strong, he forgot to breathe for a minute.

When he had it under control he moved his hand, explored some more. When he grazed a scar, he glanced down at her.

'Tell me what happened here.'

She tensed and he pressed his mouth against her palm again. 'Everything, Jasmine. I want to know everything. Before and after Stephen.'

Indecision blazed in her eyes for several seconds before she exhaled.

'Have you heard the saying that some people are just born bad?'

She shook her head at his frown and continued. 'For a long time I believed I was one of them. You know how my mother handled our situation. I just kept rebelling whenever I could. I think I wanted my mother to *see* me, deal with me. When she pretended like I didn't exist, I turned truant at a young age. Fell in with the wrong crowd.'

'What happened?'

'I just…spiralled out of control for a long time.'

'You were trying to get yourself heard the best way you could.'

'That's no excuse. I was a brat with a mother who didn't care whether she lived or died and I lashed out.'

'That's not the end of your story though, obviously.' He trailed his mouth over her palm again.

'No.' She shivered in his arms. He reached for a cashmere throw next to the fireplace and settled it over them. She snuggled into him and that alien feeling in his chest expanded wider. 'You remember that turf war I told you about?'

Reyes nodded.

'*I* was the turf they were fighting over. It happened a few months after I came out of juvie. Each side wanted me to join their gang. I seriously considered it. But I knew I would be burying my pain with destruction. So I refused, and all hell broke loose.'

He reared up and stared down at her. '*Dios.* How did you get out of that?'

'I let myself be arrested again. I reckoned the police station was a safer place than the street. It was where I met Stephen. He was an MP then, touring the police station and I...' She stopped and grimaced.

'You what?'

A dull flush crept up her cheeks. 'I may have tripped him up when he walked past me.'

He couldn't help his smile. She answered with one of her own. Unable to resist, Reyes kissed her. When he lifted his head, she was breathless and her delicious mouth was swollen. 'I presume that got his attention?'

She nodded. 'He could've filed charges against me for assault. Instead bailed me out and he took me out for a coffee. We talked for hours. He delivered me home and met my mother. Then he started visiting us every week. A few months later I started taking on the gangs myself. But instead of knives and guns, I used words. I managed to mediate a truce between them and even extracted a promise from the leaders not to recruit children to run drugs for them.'

'That's where you got your passion for mediation from?' he asked.

'Yes. I returned to school, made good grades and got my

first job at twenty-one. Stephen married my mother, and I guess the rest is history.' Her eyes met his and shifted away. 'Until Rio, that is. I'm so sorry about that, Reyes.'

Catching her chin with his finger, he tilted her face. 'I know you are. I forgive you. I judged you harshly before I knew the truth behind your actions. You tried to protect your family the only way you knew how.'

'But I ended up making things worse for you and your people.'

'You're here now, helping to fix it. That matters to me. With a new council in place, Mendez will no longer be able to play his games. The route may have been unfortunate, but perhaps it achieved something positive in the end. So from now on, we'll consider Rio another lesson we'll both learn from. Agreed?'

'Agreed,' she replied tremulously.

He brushed away the tears forming in her eyes. His head swimming with sensations he could barely grapple with, Reyes slanted his mouth over hers. When he was kissing her like this, he didn't have to think. Didn't have to wonder why he craved her even more with each kiss, each heartbeat.

He didn't have to wonder why he wished they were already married and this were their honeymoon.

A stomach growled. He raised his head. 'I believe that was you.'

She grimaced. 'Jet lag kept me asleep through lunch, and I think we missed dinner.'

Reyes reached for his discarded trousers and took out his phone. He sent his chef the appropriate instructions and hung up.

'Dinner is coming to us?' A smile that seemed to grow more breathtaking each time curved her lips.

'*Sí*. The perks of being a prince. You will command equal power once you're my princess.'

A shadow passed over her face. He wanted to demand to know the reason behind it. Something stopped him.

Her fingers drifted over his brow and down to his cheek. 'What will we do after we eat?'

'I will bathe you and you will let me explore the rest of your scars.'

Jasmine woke in the middle of night. Although the bedroom in the wedding-cake house where they'd relocated to boasted a fire, Reyes hadn't lit it when he'd carried her in. They'd had more urgent things in mind.

Now the room had cooled and she shivered. Glancing down, she realised why. The covers had slipped to the floor and the only things keeping her warm were Reyes's muscular thigh and arm. Which left the rest of her body chilled.

Carefully sliding away, she picked up the nearest sheet and walked into the bathroom.

After using it, she came back to the bed.

Reyes was snoring softly, his face even more relaxed in sleep than it'd been this evening. A lock of hair had fallen over his brow and she itched to smooth it away but stopped herself.

Over and over tonight, her heart had filled to bursting when he'd made love to her. Somewhere around midnight, she'd finally admitted that she'd fallen in love with the Crown Prince of Santo Sierra.

She loved a man who had had his heart broken, not just by one woman, but by two. And while Anaïs's betrayal had been short-term, his mother's had gone on for years.

Her heart stuttered and tears prickled her eyes. He stirred in his sleep.

She turned away and walked quickly out of the bedroom before he woke. She couldn't risk him seeing her expression. He'd been too adept at reading her moods lately. She couldn't afford to let him see that, while she was certain he'd love their baby, she could foresee herself yearning for a love he could never give her.

Going to the window, she gazed out at the twinkling lights

of San Domenica. This place was now her home, for better or worse.

She intended to do everything in her power to make sure it was the better.

She was going from delinquent to princess. Was she being selfish in asking for the icing on the cake?

Yes! She wanted it all.

Tears slipped down her cheeks before she could stop them.

'You're crying. Tell me why.'

She whirled around.

Reyes stood a few feet away, dressed in only his boxers, intense eyes scouring her face.

'I wasn't crying.'

One eyebrow was raised at her wet cheeks. 'Unless it's raining in here and I'm not aware of it, I beg to differ.'

'I never cry. Tears are for the weak.'

His eyes narrowed. 'Who told you that?'

'A gang leader years ago.' She shook her head. 'I'm sorry. That whole trip down memory lane has dredged up things I'd rather forget.'

He stepped closer, cupped her cheeks. 'And that's what woke you?'

About to nod and let that assumption hold, she hesitated. And spoke the words that scrapped up from her shredding heart. 'Are you sure you're making the right choice, Reyes? Not for your people, but for you?'

His eyes grew wary. 'Why the sudden introspection?'

'I know we're only doing this primarily for the baby, and for your people. But we'll be in this marriage, too.'

Jaw clenching, he paced in tight circles in front of her. 'What are you saying?'

'That you need to be sure before we take a step we can't retrace.'

He froze. His nostrils flared as he jerked his fingers through his hair. 'What's going on, Jasmine? Why are you crying? Are you having second thoughts?'

She swiped at her cheeks and grappled with what to say. Settling on a half truth, she met his gaze. Slowly, she nodded. 'Yes, and I think deep down you probably are, too.'

His brows clamped together. 'Don't put words in my mouth.'

Jasmine would've given anything not to utter the words. 'Then tell me in your own words.'

He stared at her for a long time. Then shook his head. 'I don't have the luxury of being whimsical about this situation. It is what it is.'

The vice tightened around her heart. 'What about love, Reyes? Surely you have a view on whether you want love in your life or not?'

His hand slashed through the air. 'My father married for love. Look where that got him.'

'Are you saying if you fell in love and were loved back, it wouldn't be enough for you?'

'I'm saying love is never equal, no matter what anyone says. Someone always loves more, and that person has the most to lose.' Shadows flickered in his eyes before he turned to pace the room again.

Her beautiful eyes clouded. 'You really believe that, don't you?'

Striding to her, he grabbed her arms. 'I don't believe in fairy tales. And my reality speaks for itself.'

She pushed out of his arms and padded to the window. Tugging the sheet closer, she wrapped her arms around herself.

Reyes watched her, the action both angering and disturbing him. 'Jasmine?'

After a moment, she turned. 'How is your father?'

He frowned, struggling to keep up with everything she was throwing at him.

Waking up to find her gone, he'd had a chilling sense of déjà vu, before he'd remembered he was back home, in a place where Jasmine wouldn't be able to escape him easily. Except she was trying now. The woman he'd gone to sleep certain of spending the rest of his life with was having second thoughts.

And probing subjects he didn't want to discuss. Yet he found himself answering. 'As well as he can be considering his heart and organs are days away from failing.' The throb of pain the thought brought made his breath catch. His father had had a good day today. Straight after his council meeting, Reyes had gone to see him. They'd talked for a full hour, during which Reyes had stumbled over himself in his plea for his father's forgiveness for treating him so harshly.

His father had merely smiled and said, 'Finally, you love,' before he'd fallen asleep.

'Can he speak?' Jasmine asked.

He shoved a hand through his hair. 'A few words when the medication isn't strong enough to make him sleepy.'

She nodded. 'Can you do me a favour? The next time you see him, ask him if he'd do it all over again. Love your mother with unconditional love.'

His insides clenched and he exhaled. 'I don't need to ask him. I know he would.'

'Do you think that's foolish? Those brief moments of happiness to balance the pain and the betrayal?'

'Jasmine—'

'Just humour me. You have no idea how many times I wished for my mother to just tell me she loved me, or for her to remember it was my birthday without the shopkeeper down the road having to remind her. Was it always that bad between your parents?'

Reyes thought back to birthdays, skiing holidays, family gatherings. His mother had made an effort on those rare occasions. Those were the happiest he'd seen his father. But as with all things, the happy moments were fleeting, the painful moments lingering the longest.

He shook his head. 'It wasn't, no. But it was a life…so-called *love*…without trust and respect. And to me that's no life at all. Do you not agree?'

Her shoulders slumped. A flare of panic lit his insides.

'It doesn't really matter what I think, does it? You've made up your mind. We have a wedding to plan and a baby to look forward to.'

She was staying. The panic should've abated, yet it escalated. 'We can make this work, Jasmine.'

Her dejection grew even more palpable. 'Reyes—'

He cupped her shoulders. 'We *will* make it work. That is my edict.'

Her chin rose and although her eyes filled with more tears, they didn't spill. But they spiked her lashes and clung like tiny diamonds.

'I know you're the Crown Prince, possibly soon to be King, but I'm really tired of you ordering me around like I'm some type of minion. Get over yourself already.'

She flung away from him, trailed the sheet to the bedroom and then reversed her trajectory back to the living room to snatch up her gown.

Watching her try to manoeuvre the dress on while keeping hold of the sheet tugged a reluctant smile from his lips, despite his churning feelings.

She saw it and glared at him. 'You think this is funny?'

'Firstly, I don't think I've ever been told to get over myself before. Secondly, I suggest you stop hopping around like that before you fall over and break a bone. Or worse.'

'*Firstly*, I think it's high time someone told you to get over yourself. Secondly—' She yanked the dress up, dropped the sheet, and tripped over her feet. He lunged forward, all mirth gone from the situation, and caught her in his arms.

'You can let me go now. I'm done putting my dress on.'

His chest tightened again, harder than before. 'And where do you propose going at three in the morning?'

'Back to the palace, of course.'

'No. If you're upset we'll talk about it now.'

That look of inevitable acceptance of defeat crossed her face again. *Dios*, what was going on? 'You can't will something into place that doesn't exist, Reyes.'

'What are you talking about?'

'We're only marrying because of the baby. I think we should focus on that and not fool ourselves into thinking this can ever be something more, okay?'

Something more. A part of him wanted that. The part that wanted to say *to hell with everything* and jump in blind. But he couldn't afford to do that. This time the stakes were much too high. 'Jasmine, I can't give you what—'

She held up her hand and shook her head. 'I know. I'm not what you wanted. You don't need to spell it out.' She turned away. 'I'd really like to return to the palace now, please.'

He dressed. Made sure she was warm enough in the pre-dawn air as he settled her into the buggy. All the while feeling terrified that he had lost the most important battle of his life.

CHAPTER SEVENTEEN

THEY WERE MARRIED two days later in the largest cathedral in Santo Sierra. Church bells tolled at the strike of midday and white doves were released in commemoration of the historic event. Quite how the palace staff had managed to gather and accommodate world leaders and royalty in such a short space of time would've blown Jasmine's mind, had she not been in a continued state of numb shock.

Stephen and her mother had flown in this morning on Reyes's jet, and, although Jasmine had had a hard time managing her mother's questions and tearful exclamations of how beautiful Jasmine looked, she was thankful for their presence. They were literally two familiar faces in a multitude of strangers.

Her mother was riding in the second car with Isabella, while Jasmine rode to the cathedral in the back of a Rolls-Royce Phantom. Beside her, Stephen enumerated the many luxuries of the car. Jasmine nodded absently, too preoccupied with not throwing up over her astonishingly beautiful gown to answer.

All too soon, they arrived at the church. A dozen ten-year-old pageboys lined either side of the royal-blue carpet that led to the aisle, each one holding up a jewelled-hilted sword that signified the twelve generations since Reyes's ancestors had ruled Santo Sierra.

Jasmine gripped Stephen's arm as her stepfather led her down the aisle. She tried to pin a smile on her face as the sea of faces on either side of the aisle gawped at her with unbridled curiosity.

The surprise wedding and unconfirmed reports of a possible pregnancy had sent the world's media wild. The press office's *no comment* on the subject had been taken as tacit confirmation.

'Almost there, my darling,' Stephen murmured. His reassurance calmed her nerves, helping her to focus on her destination.

The top of the aisle, where Reyes waited. She couldn't see his face clearly through her lace veil, but his imposing figure was hard to miss. Dressed in formal military regalia complete with shoulder tassels, sash and sword, he looked more dashing than any man had the right to look.

The butterflies in her stomach multiplied.

Since their night at the wedding-cake house, she'd seen him for less than a handful of minutes. Each time, he'd been reserved to the point of being curt. At their last meeting, he'd presented her with an engagement ring belonging to his grandmother. The stunning baguette diamond ring she now wore on her right hand, according to protocol, was flanked by two further teardrop diamonds and completed in a platinum band.

Reyes had stopped only to ask whether she liked it before, after her startled nod, he'd walked away.

She couldn't help but think that her probing questions about love had twigged him to her feelings for him. Feelings he didn't welcome.

All through the many fittings and wedding protocol, she hadn't been able to dismiss the knowledge that Reyes would never love her, no matter how much she tried. Again and again she recalled the look on his face when she'd blurted out that damning statement on the plane. A statement he hadn't so far denied.

Stephen eased her hand from his arm, and she realised they'd reached the steps of the altar. Eyes damp, her stepfather gazed down at her. 'I'm so proud of, my dear. So very proud,' he murmured. 'You're the daughter I wished for, and I hope you'll forgive me for not always being the father I could've been.'

She knew he was referring to the business with Joaquin.

Her throat clogged and she blinked back her own tears. 'There's nothing to forgive. Absolutely nothing,' she whispered back.

His own eyes brimming with tears, Stephen placed her hand on the gloved hand Reyes held out.

She searched Reyes's face, and her heart dropped. Nothing in his demeanour showed he was happy to be here. He flinched when a muted roar sounded from outside where the crowd was watching the ceremony on giant screens.

Intent on discovering a hint of emotion that would abate the fear beating beneath her breast, she stepped closer to him.

A discreet cough sounded half a step behind her. She turned to find a teenage usher holding out a polished silver tray. Flustered, Jasmine placed her bouquet on it, and tried to ignore the hushed murmuring behind her.

Reyes squeezed her hand. Heart lifting, she glanced at him. But he was staring straight ahead, his chiselled profile holding no signs of tenderness.

They exchanged vows in Spanish and English, with the sermon and following register signing also conducted in both languages.

When the priest urged Reyes to kiss his bride, his lips barely warmed hers for a moment before he stepped back.

Through it all, Jasmine smiled, and felt her heart break into tiny pieces. She'd fallen in love with a man who she had a soul-deep suspicion would never love her back.

A cheer from the thousands of subjects lining the streets roused Jasmine from her dazed state. Her hand tightened on Reyes's arm as he helped her into the gilt-framed glass carriage.

'Smile, *querida*. Anyone would think you were attending a funeral, not your own wedding.'

Plastering a smile on her face, she waved to the crowd. 'I haven't seen anything of you in the past two days,' she muttered from the side of her lips.

Reyes lifted his hand in acknowledgement of the crowd.

'And neither will you be seeing me for the coming weeks. I'm going to be very busy. I assume you saw Mendez among the guests?'

The heart that had squeezed painfully at his first words lurched in anxiety at the reference to Mendez. 'Yes, I did.'

'I sent the opening salvo yesterday. He's desperate to recommence talks.'

She continued to wave as she'd been instructed and glanced at Reyes from the corner of her eye. 'What about the new council? Will they back you?'

'Yes, I have people in place I trust. I don't intend to stop until a new treaty is signed.'

She nodded, feeling miserable inside. Trust was important. Would he ever trust her enough to let himself feel more for her?

Not likely.

Her hand drooped. Thankfully, they were going through a long archway that connected San Domenica to the palace, where the wedding banquet was being held.

'Are you all right?'

Her breath huffed out before she could stop it. 'I'm an ex-juvenile delinquent who's just been crowned Princess of one of the most influential kingdoms in the world. I'm very, very far from all right.'

She startled as he picked up her free hand and placed it on his thigh. 'You've overcome the adversities thrust at you many times before. You'll rise to the challenge this time, too.'

Her limbs weakened and, against her better judgement, hope sprang in her chest. It bloomed when he picked up her hand and kissed the back of it.

The roar vibrated against the glass, and she became painfully aware of the reason for the gesture. Pain slammed into her. She couldn't pull away, not without thousands of eyes witnessing the withdrawal.

She kept the smile on her face until she feared her jaw would crack. 'So the honeymoon is over even before the ink has dried on the marriage certificate?' she demanded waspishly.

His eyes gleamed. 'I'm sure you'll agree that ours hasn't been a straightforward route to the altar.'

If it hadn't been for the baby, they wouldn't have found themselves in front of an altar at all. 'No. I guess not.'

His lips pursed, an infinitesimal motion no one else would've caught. But she saw it.

'Can I suggest, however, that we make the best of it?'

When his gaze dropped to her stomach, and an intense emotion passed over his face, Jasmine's world greyed further.

'Of course.'

She tried to breathe, but there was little room in her wedding dress for such frivolities. The lace-and-satin gown cupped her breast and torso and dropped to flare in a long dress and train. Isabella had called every fashion house in Europe and had started a bidding war on who would design the Crown Princess's wedding gown. The two-day deadline hadn't daunted even one of them.

Jasmine had finally settled on a Milanese couturier who'd worked magic with fabric right before her eyes. The material was heavy without being oppressive and the lace provided her with means of keeping cool in the hot Santo Sierran sun.

Now her crown was a different story. It weighed a ton, decorated as it was with ninety-nine diamonds, rubies and emeralds.

She touched it, felt the sharp bumps of precious gems beneath her fingers, and hysterical laughter bubbled from her throat. 'Is it true the crown designer stopped at ninety-nine because the palace decreed at the time that a hundred was too ostentatious?'

One corner of his mouth lifted. 'You've been learning Santo Sierra history.'

'I thought I should, seeing as I have no choice now.'

His smile dimmed. '*Sí*, we all have our crosses to bear.'

* * *

The wedding banquet carried on much like the wedding. Except where several priests muttered homilies, Jasmine had to sit through several speeches from well-wishers from around the world.

Numerous toasts were also raised in honour of the absent king, whom she'd met for the first time that morning.

So very like his son in stature, but with a defeated look in his eyes that made him seem...*less*. He'd haltingly given them their blessing before his medication had kicked in again.

She'd watched Reyes kiss his father's forehead with tears trapped in her throat. The love between father and son had been palpable, and Jasmine could just imagine what the turbulent period had done to them.

The clear love in his eyes when he gazed down at his father had given her a little more hope. Hope that was very quickly dwindling as the distance between them grew with each hour.

She smiled for a solid hour. Then smiled some more. Finally, she couldn't stand it any more. They'd finished with the formalities and those guests who wished it were getting into the dancing session of the evening.

Jasmine rose.

'I'm going to bed.'

Reyes glanced up from where he'd been in deep conversation with one of his advisors. Rising, too, he tucked her arm through his.

'I'll escort you.'

She shook her head. 'You don't need to—'

'*Sí*, I do.' The implacable dominance behind the words shut her up.

As they mounted the stairs her heart began to flutter.

Everything had gone at such a fast and furious pace, she hadn't thought to the wedding night.

Liar.

She'd thought of nothing *but* the wedding night since she

woke this morning, and terrified herself with different scenarios, most of which had ended with her going to bed alone.

Now, as she walked beside Reyes…her *husband*…she allowed herself to believe everything would be all right.

They reached their door and he raised her hand to his mouth,
kissed the back of it. 'I've arranged for two of the servants to
help you with your gown. Sleep well, *querida*.'

CHAPTER EIGHTEEN

One month later...

JASMINE WAS EXHAUSTED. Her feet ached and a headache throbbed behind her left ear. Relaxing in the air-conditioned car that was taking her back to the palace, she massaged her nape.

The four hours she'd been scheduled to teach her mediation class at Santo Sierra's municipal college had stretched to six. Not because her students were dying to learn everything she could teach them about mediation.

No. She'd been delayed because her young students had been fascinated about what it was like to be Queen.

Hysteria rose in her chest. She'd been Crown Princess for a pathetically short time before the King's sudden decline in health and subsequent death had propelled Reyes onto the throne and her into being Queen.

Beyond that, nothing had changed in her world. Jasmine had wanted to rip the rose-coloured glasses from her students' eyes. Tell them to find and settle for unconditional love and nothing else.

They wouldn't have believed her, though, even if she'd managed to utter the words. They all believed she'd captured the world's most eligible man and brought him to his knees after a whirlwind romance. Just as she, Reyes and his councillors had planned in San Estrela what felt like a lifetime ago.

What they didn't know was that she hadn't seen her husband for two weeks and she hadn't shared his bed since the night they'd spent at the wedding-cake house.

He'd spent the days leading up to his father's death in a vigil by King Carlos's bed with Isabella. Jasmine had berated herself for feeling left out.

Then, after the King's passing, they'd had to deal with the arduous protocol of the coronation. Reyes had accepted his duties as King with gravity and pride, but the result had been an even greater distance between them as he'd dived headlong into securing economic ties he'd fought so hard for.

Jasmine understood the duties that being King demanded. And yet she couldn't help but think her husband was using them as a perfect excuse to stay away from her.

She had woken up one night two weeks ago to find him in bed with her, his hand spread over her flat belly. Choking back tears, she'd placed her hand over his and gone back to sleep, her heart lifting with the hope that maybe they'd turned a corner.

She'd awakened hours later to an empty, cold half of the bed.

Jasmine hadn't thought a heart could shatter into tinier pieces until that moment.

The limo turned onto the mile-long drive leading to the palace.

Unable to face the palace and her lonely suite, she pressed the intercom on the armrest that connected to the driver. 'Can you take me round to the other house, please?'

Her driver glanced sharply at her. 'But, Your Majesty, it's Thursday today, not Friday.'

Jasmine nodded. 'I know, Raul. Take me there anyway.'

'Of course. As you wish, Your Majesty,' he replied deferentially.

She'd started going to the small house every Friday and staying the night. If she'd had a choice, Jasmine would've moved into the adorable little house. But considering she needed an armed escort wherever she went, she couldn't subject her guards to nightly patrols in the cold. So she'd restricted her visits to once a week. But this week, she might make it two nights...

Reyes was off hammering out the last terms of the new trade treaty, and Isabella had left for Milan this morning to consult over her autumn/winter wardrobe.

She'd urged Jasmine to go along with her, but she hadn't

been in the mood. Besides, by the time winter rolled around she would be in the late stages of pregnancy.

Leaning her head back, she rubbed her hand over her belly. The morning sickness had finally waned and, according to the team of doctors tending her, both she and the baby were healthy.

In a way, she understood how anyone on the outside would believe her world was rosy. She had everything her heart could wish for...

Except a husband who loved her even a fraction as hopelessly as she loved him.

They arrived at the house. Her door opened and Raul helped her out. She smiled and stepped out. 'Don't worry about informing the palace. I'll let them know when I get inside.'

'Yes, Your Majesty.'

She wanted to ask him to call her Jasmine. But protocol was protocol. She could go inside her little house, pretend she was at her flat in London for a while, but the palace, the Santo Sierran people who'd welcomed her wholeheartedly, and her absentee husband would still be her reality when she stepped out again.

Jasmine climbed the steps into the house and shut the door behind her. Ten minutes later, clutching a bowl of warm popcorn and a bottle of water, she plopped herself down in front of the TV and activated the chess game she'd started last week.

She was in the middle of checkmating *GrandChessMaster231* when the door burst open.

Her heart somersaulted, then banged against her ribs. 'Reyes!'

'Do you know how long the staff have been looking for you?' he burst out.

She rose on shaky feet, the unexpected sight of him rendering her senses stupid. 'But I...Raul knew where I was. I told him...' She stopped and grimaced.

'You told him what?' he demanded.

'I told him not to bother telling the palace staff where I was because I would ring them. I forgot.'

He kicked the door shut and clawed both hands through his hair. 'Raul discovered a slow puncture after he dropped you off so he went straight to the garage without stopping at the palace. The staff have been searching for you for the past four hours, Jasmine.'

'I'm sorry, I didn't think... I just wanted to be on my own for a little while.'

He dropped his hands, took a good look around the room, before he zeroed in on her again. This time, his gaze travelled from her head to her toes and back again. His hands slowly curled and uncurled at his sides.

'I've been told you spend a lot of time in here.'

She shrugged and considered sitting back down before her weak knees gave way. But sitting down would make Reyes's presence more overwhelming. So she settled for propping herself on the armrest.

'When did you get back?'

'This afternoon.'

They stared at each other a full minute before she managed to tear her gaze away. 'How was your trip?'

He scowled. 'I don't want to talk about my trip. Why have you not been sleeping in our bed?'

The bitter laugh escaped before she could stop it. 'It's not *our* bed, Reyes. I sleep in it alone, even when you're in Santo Sierra...even when we're under the same roof, I sleep alone. I'm sorry I worried the staff but you know where I am now, so you can go back to...wherever you came from.'

He looked stunned at her outburst. Jasmine wanted to laugh again, but she couldn't trust that it wouldn't emerge a sob.

She plopped herself down on the sofa and released the pause button.

After several minutes, he sat down beside her. Awareness of him crawled all over her body. But she didn't dare look at him or she was afraid she'd beg him to stay. Beg him to love her. While she wasn't afraid of begging, she was terrified of the rejection.

Was it her imagination or had he moved closer?

'Jasmine, we need to talk.'

Her hands shook. 'So talk.'

He shifted his gaze from her face to the screen. Or so she thought until his breath caressed her ear. 'Can I make a wager, *por favor*?' he asked, his tone rough.

'Can I stop you?'

'Ditch *GrandChessMaster231*. Play me. For every game I win, you stop and listen to me for three minutes.'

Her pulse tripped over itself. Her head started to turn, but she snapped her gaze back to the screen. 'Okay.'

He beat her at the first game in less than five minutes.

'What did you—'

His lips took hers. It was thorough, hungry, incandescent. Even as her mind reeled Jasmine's lips clung to his, already desperate for the pleasure only he could provide. The pleasure she'd missed more than breathing. Her nerveless fingers let go when he tugged the control from her grasp and dropped it on the floor, all without taking his mouth from hers.

He pulled away from her, his breathing ragged. 'I have two minutes remaining. Why do you not sleep in our bed, *mi corazón*?' he rasped.

'Because…because you're not in it,' she choked out. 'It's cold and lonely without you, and I can't stand it.'

He nodded solemnly, then captured her lips in another scorching kiss. Freeing her when his time was up, he picked up the control and handed it back to her.

He won the next game, too. Another bone-melting kiss, followed by a long look into her eyes. 'If I told you I missed you every day I was away from you, would you believe me?' His voice was low, deep. Almost prayerful.

'No.'

The hand in her hair trembled. 'I deserve that. I know I've behaved badly, have approached things the wrong way—'

'Your time's up.' She handed him his control.

She had burning questions of her own, so Jasmine put all her effort into winning the next level.

Her control fell from her fingers. 'You scheduled sex with your other candidates. But you left me, your wife—'

'My queen,' he growled.

'Your queen, to sleep in our marriage bed alone. Why? Am I so unlovable?'

He squeezed his eyes shut for a split second. 'You are far from unlovable, *querida*. It was me. I was afraid.'

She looked at him, stunned. 'Afraid of what?'

'The last time we were in this house together, you tried to get out of marrying me. I was afraid you'd change your mind about staying with me. We didn't have to get married in three days. I rushed it because I didn't want to let you go. I couldn't see past the fact that you'd woken up in the middle of the night determined to leave me. I'd already jumped on the pregnancy to make you my bride—'

She gasped. 'You wanted to marry me before you knew I was pregnant?'

'I dismissed perfectly good candidates because they were not you. I didn't want to admit it to myself, but I couldn't see any of them as my wife. None of them touched me the way you did. When the pregnancy presented itself as an option for me keeping you, I took it.'

The timer on the screen beeped. They both ignored it.

Tears filled her eyes. He brushed them away with his fingers.

'I thought you were only with me because of the baby.'

He looked down at her belly, then back at her. 'I love our child more than I can adequately put into words. I was overwhelmed with terror that you'd wake up in the middle of the night and ask for your freedom.'

Her mouth wobbled before she pursed her lips. 'And the night you came to me?'

'I came to tell you that Joaquin Esteban had been arrested.'

She gasped. 'What?'

'Mendez handed him over as part of our agreement. If I have anything to do with it, Esteban won't see the light of day again.'

Tears threatened. She blinked them away. 'So you came to tell me…and?'

'You looked so beautiful. I couldn't stay away. I missed you so much I couldn't breathe, never mind sleep. I planned to leave a note and be gone before you realised I was there. Leaving you ripped me apart. After that I didn't want to put myself through it again…so I used my duties as an excuse to stay away.'

A deep tremble shook her. 'Oh, Reyes.'

The timer beeped again.

She asked the question burning its way through her heart. 'Why are you here now, Reyes?'

'Because staying away from you is killing me. I need to be with you. With our baby. Loving you, protecting you both.' He started to reach for her.

She pulled back. 'Loving me?'

He closed his eyes. '*Dios*. This wasn't how I intended it to go—'

'Stop trying to wrap everything perfectly and just tell me how you feel!'

'I love you.' He exhaled, then struggled to catch his breath again. 'You blew me away that first night in Rio. I went to sleep thinking I could have found the one, even though I wasn't looking for you or even dreaming that the overwhelming feelings I felt for you existed. I let how I felt about my mother and Anaïs cloud my judgement so I could hate you for what you did. Even after I understood your motivation I was too scared to let you in.

'But you wormed your way in anyway. I admire your courage, your intelligence. My people love you already and it's been mere weeks since you entered their lives.'

Jasmine smiled. 'I love Santo Sierra. I've loved your home and its people since I stepped off the plane, Reyes. And I adore its king. When he's not breaking my heart by staying away from me for weeks on end.'

He caught her to him and smothered her with long, breath-stealing kisses. 'Your king is back. He will never leave your side again.' He spread his hand over her belly again the way he'd done, painfully briefly, weeks ago. 'He will never leave either of you. Ever again.'

With a flick of his finger, he turned the screen off. When he pulled his shirt over his head, she could barely keep from crying with joy. 'Reyes…'

'I'm here, *querida*,' he rasped.

Strong hands reached for her, lifting her up and carrying her into the bedroom. About to kiss him back, she paused. 'Did you bring any guards with you?'

A look, almost of regret, passed over his face. '*Sí*, it's protocol. But they know not to disturb us, even when you scream with passion. Now, where was I?'

The look in his eyes set off spirals of excitement through her. Feeling almost wanton, she slowly licked her tongue over her upper lip. 'Somewhere here, I think.'

She expected his customary growl, a sound she'd become accustomed to when he was fully aroused. Not this time. His eyes fixed on hers, he slowly inhaled, taking in her scent, imprinting her on his senses.

Jasmine found that even more enthralling than his growl and she watched, fascinated, as his chest expanded on his breath. Slowly he breathed out. 'I don't know what it is about you, Jasmine Navarre, but you captivate me. I might even go as far as to say I'm completely obsessed by you.'

Her breath stalled in her throat. 'Stay that way, and we won't have a problem at all.'

'I love you, my queen.'

'I love you, Reyes.'

His eyes misted. Then he cleared his throat. 'No more talking.'

His kiss was hard, possessive, sucking out every last ounce

of sanity from her as he unleashed the raw power of his arousal. He broke from her mouth to let her inhale a mere breath before he was back again, demanding. And receiving the unfettered response she couldn't hide.

Jasmine touched. Stroked. Nearly wept with delight at the sheer pleasure touching Reyes brought her. And everywhere she touched his skin seemed to react, to heat, bunch and flex, as if his every nerve ending was attuned to her.

That thought only served to increase her bliss. He pulled away for a moment. 'I know you'll berate me if I ruin your precious shirt, so I'll let you take it off.'

She wanted to tell him she didn't care if he ripped her shirt to shreds! But no way would she be able to articulate those words, not when her brain was too busy devouring the solid, sculpted lines of his naked torso. With shaking fingers, she divested herself of her shirt, letting it fall to the ground unheeded.

She arched her back, reached for her bra.

He growled low in his throat.

'I love that sound.'

'I growl only for you, *mi amor*. Always and for ever.'

* * * * *